/
M3625t

# TEN KIDS,
# NO·PETS

# TEN KIDS, NO PETS

*Ann M. Martin*

HOLIDAY HOUSE / NEW YORK

Library of Congress Cataloging-in-Publication Data

Martin, Ann M.
Ten kids, no pets.

SUMMARY: The ten Rosso children, spaced a year apart
and named alphabetically, find their life rambunctious
and exciting when their family leaves New York City
for a big old farmhouse and new friends.
    [1. Family life—Fiction. 2. Country life—
Fiction.] I. Title.
PZ7.M3567585Te   1988    [Fic]    87-25206
ISBN 0-8234-0691-1

For my parents,
who raised
two kids,
nine cats,
several mice,
a litter of hamsters,
two guinea pigs,
and some fish and turtles

# CONTENTS

| | | |
|---|---|---|
| 1: | Abigail | 3 |
| 2: | Calandra | 21 |
| 3: | Ira | 36 |
| 4: | Dagwood | 52 |
| 5: | Gardenia | 71 |
| 6: | Janthina | 87 |
| 7: | Eberhard | 103 |
| 8: | Hannah | 119 |
| 9: | Faustine | 134 |
| 10: | Bainbridge | 150 |
| 11: | Zsa Zsa or Zuriel | 167 |

# TEN KIDS,
# NO PETS

# CHAPTER ONE
# *ABIGAIL*

"Abbie, fix my hair . . . *please?*"

"Abbie, I need you!"

"Abbie, I can't move my suitcase! It's too heavy."

Abbie Rosso closed her eyes for a moment. She was not the mother of all of these children. She was only their big sister.

"Kids! The moving van is almost loaded up." Mrs. Rosso ran breathlessly into the bedroom. "Are you sure there's nothing left anywhere? In the closets? In a cupboard?"

Abbie's mother was a sight. August was not a good time of year to move. Especially not to move out of hot, grimy New York City.

"Mom, take that dust rag off your head," Abbie

whispered loudly. "Someone might see you."

"Plenty of people have already seen me," replied Mrs. Rosso. (Abbie groaned.) "Now please, kids. Give me some help here. You're sure nothing's left behind? If we don't pack it now, it'll stay in New York forever."

"There's nothing!" exclaimed Woody, sounding exasperated.

"Nothing, nothing, nothing," added Jan, hopping from one foot to the other.

"Did you *check?*" asked Mrs. Rosso.

"Nope," said Woody.

"*I* did," said Bainbridge. He was the oldest of the boys. "It's okay, Mom. The movers got everything. I'm positive."

"Thank you." Mrs. Rosso glanced out the window at the moving van three floors below. Then she left the bedroom, taking a suitcase with her.

"I can't believe we are actually moving," said Abbie, shaking her head. She wasn't speaking to anyone in particular, and none of her nine brothers and sisters answered her. What did she expect? It was moving day. They were excited. Every single one of the Rossos wanted to move to the big farmhouse in New Jersey—except Abbie.

Abbie wandered into the bedroom she had shared with Candy and the twins. It wasn't a very big room, and it had always been a mess, between Candy's books and Faustine and Gardenia's nature collection, but it had been the room she had grown up in. More important, the room was in New York, which was where Abbie wanted to stay.

Abbie was fourteen. She would be starting high school in a month. She had friends—lots of them—in New York. And they weren't all girls, either. Lately, Roddy Howard had been calling her on the phone. And once, when she'd been sitting in front of her building watching Ira and Jan, the Mr. Softee ice-cream truck had come by, and Josh Freeberg from the building next door had bought Abbie a toasted almond popsicle. Abbie was pretty sure she wouldn't hear from Roddy or Josh after today.

"That's mine! Give it back!"

"No, it's mine! I claim it!"

Abbie could hear a fight starting in the next room. By the sound of things it was going to be a doozy. Bainbridge was there, and he might break it up—or he might not. Since Abbie was the oldest of all the kids, she felt it was her duty to keep them in line.

Abbie dashed into the room that had been the little kids' bedroom. Hannah, who was eight, was tussling with Jan, who was six, over a pen.

"Hannah! Janthina!" cried Abbie. She separated them, then stood between them with her hands on her hips. She took the pen from Hannah. "Who started this?" she asked.

"She did!" the girls exclaimed, pointing at each other.

Bainbridge stepped in. "Jan found the pen under the radiator. Hannah says she lost it last winter."

"I can't believe you guys are fighting over a ball-point pen," said Abbie.

"There's nothing else to fight over," replied Hannah, glancing around the bare room.

The other kids laughed. Hannah could usually make them do that.

"Well, I'll keep it for now," said Abbie. She stuck it in the back pocket of her jeans. "When we get to New Jersey, we'll decide what to do with it."

Footsteps sounded in the hallway outside the bedrooms. Mr. Rosso strode into the room where Abbie and her brothers and sisters were waiting with their suitcases.

"Is the van all packed?" asked Ira. Ira was seven. He was the tidiest person Abbie knew. It was important to Ira that the van not only be packed but be packed neatly.

"It's all packed," replied Mr. Rosso.

Abbie's father sat down on the windowsill. Apart from the floor, it was the only place to sit in the bare room. Looking at him, Abbie thought that her father was probably in the wrong profession. He was an advertising executive in New York, and a very respected one, from what Abbie could tell. On weekdays he wore a dark suit and a tie and polished shoes. He carried a briefcase with a fat appointment calendar in it and rode around the city in cabs, having important lunches with other businesspeople. Once he had eaten dinner with Mayor Koch.

But that Mr. Rosso wasn't the real one. The real Mr. Rosso came to life on the weekends. He wore faded blue jeans and work boots and soft, old shirts with the sleeves rolled up to his elbows. And he made furniture. That was his passion—carpentry. The Rossos had a fairly large apartment, as apartments in New York go, and Mr. Rosso had taken over one end of the kitchen for his woodworking. The arrangement was fine if you didn't mind sawdust in your soup every now and then, but Abbie's father often complained that he didn't have enough space. If he had more space, he could build bureaus and tables (and maybe one day a wall unit), instead of just chairs and bookshelves. Now that they were moving to the farmhouse, Mr. Rosso would have a whole basement to himself.

"Do you kids have everything?" asked Mr. Rosso.

Abbie's brothers and sisters nodded. Abbie thought that was a pretty funny question, coming from her father. Mr. Rosso might have been an important businessman, but at least around home, he was just like the absentminded professor in a funny old movie Abbie had once seen. He would lose things and forget things, he was completely disorganized, and his mind was always off in outer space. Once Bainbridge had found Mr. Rosso looking through a carpentry catalog in the living room.

"Dad?" he had asked.

"Hmm?"

"Is it all right if I shave my head, get a monkey, and move to Chicago?"

Mr. Rosso hadn't even glanced up. "Mm-hmm," he had replied.

Woody and Hardy, who were eleven and ten, had been listening. They had laughed so hard they'd fallen on the floor.

Mr. Rosso now continued to sit on the windowsill in the bedroom. Abbie and Bainbridge glanced at each other.

"Daddy?" said Ira. "Is it time to go?"

"What? . . . . Oh, yes. Yes, it is."

"Yoo-hoo! Where is everybody?" Mrs. Rosso called from the other end of the apartment.

Abbie blushed. She blushed every time her mother said something as embarrassing as "yoo-hoo," which was fairly often.

"We're still back here, Mom!" Abbie replied.

Mrs. Rosso entered the bedroom, and then the entire Rosso family was together. There were Abbie's parents, Abbie herself, and Bainbridge, Calandra (who was called Candy), Dagwood (Woody), Eber-

hard (Hardy), Faustine and Gardenia (or Dinnie),
Hannah, Ira, and Janthina (Jan).

There were a lot of interesting things about Abbie
and her brothers and sisters, and most of those interesting things were due to Mrs. Rosso. First of all,
Abbie's mother had decided to have all of her children
a year apart, and that was exactly what she had done.
The ten kids were like stairsteps (except for Faustine
and Dinnie, the twins, who were a sort of landing on
the stairs). Abbie was fourteen, Bainbridge was thirteen, Candy was twelve, Woody was eleven, Hardy
was ten, Faustine and Dinnie were nine, Hannah was
eight, Ira was seven, and Jan was six.

Then there was the business of their names. It was
apparent to most people that some of the kids had
highly unusual names. It was apparent to a few people that the kids had been named in alphabetical
order—*A* for Abigail, *B* for Bainbridge. . . . What nobody outside the family knew was just how Mrs.
Rosso had chosen those particular names. She had a
system for naming her children, just as she had a system for almost everything she did.

Mrs. Rosso liked systems and rules. Her rules were
not the no-sweets-before-dinner or the no-Saturday-
morning-cartoons kinds of rules. They were rules that
involved running the house, such as glasses must be
put in the cupboards according to height. Or books,
records, and tapes must be shelved in alphabetical

order. Or clean clothes must always be put away at the bottom of the pile so that the clothes on top were used first. ("That way," she had explained once, "they wear out evenly.") All of her rules were designed to save time and money, two things you don't have much of in a ten-kid family.

The naming system was a simple one. Abigail was the first Rosso child, and her name was the first name on the *A* page in the girls' half of Mrs. Rosso's dog-eared book called *What Shall We Name the Baby?* Bainbridge was the second name on the *B* page in the boys' half, Calandra was the third name on the *C* page in the girls' half. This was a fine system, Abbie thought, if you didn't mind winding up with children named Eberhard and Gardenia. Abbie and Hannah and Ira were nice, normal names. Faustine and Calandra were romantic and old-fashioned-sounding. But Bainbridge? *Dagwood?* It was no wonder poor Woody got into so many fights. Maybe, Abbie thought, when they moved to the farm, the kids in Woody's new school wouldn't find out what his real name was. That was one advantage to Dagwood's awful name. He could shorten it. So could Eberhard. But Bainbridge was stuck. Luckily, he was easygoing. And for some reason, when kids found that out about him, they didn't tease him so much.

"Well, if you're all ready," said Mrs. Rosso, interrupting Abbie's thoughts, "then it's time to get into the van."

The "van" was not the moving van, of course, but the mini-van the Rossos had bought as soon as they'd bought the farmhouse. They'd traded in their little Toyota Celica, which had been fine for short drives in the city with two or three kids, for a mini-van that held all twelve of them, with room to spare.

The Rosso kids, especially the younger boys, loved the van. They tore out of the apartment and began thundering down the hall to the elevators. Mr. and Mrs. Rosso followed.

Abbie took her time. "I'll be right there, Mom," she called.

Abbie left the little kids' room and went back to her own room for one final, long look. She gazed out the window. This is the last time I'll see this view, she thought. The view was of the brick apartment building across the street, a newsstand, the Aloha Deli, and Mrs. Ho's flower shop. Abbie let her eyes drift from one to the next and back to the apartments. There was Mr. Fineman's old cat snoozing on the windowsill. Abbie had seen Puddin' there every morning for as long as she could remember. And there was Mr. Fineman himself, peering down at the Rossos and the van from behind his lace curtains. Mr. Fineman was the neighborhood spy and tattletale. No kid could get away with anything if he was at the window.

Abbie wandered out of her room and along the hall to what had been the older boys' room. She saw the dent in the wall from the time Woody had thrown a shoe at Hardy and missed. She saw the marks on the door jamb where Bainbridge had kept track of the car wrecks he'd seen from the window. Abbie's footsteps echoed woodenly as she walked through the empty rooms. Without furniture the apartment looked huge. Maybe they didn't need to move after all. They had plenty of space; why did they need more?

Abbie walked slowly through the living room and dining room and den and finally reached the front door.

She paused there, drew in a deep breath, and left the apartment. Last time, she thought, as she rode the elevator to the ground floor. My last time in our apartment building.

Abbie's eyes were assaulted by glaring sunlight, and her ears were assaulted by the shouts of her brothers and sisters as she closed the door to the building behind her.

"I want to sit in back!" Woody shouted.

"I want to ride in front, next to Daddy!" cried Jan.

"You know the rule," Mrs. Rosso said. "Biggest kids in back, littlest ones in front, in alphabetical order"—which was also age order—"and *I* sit next to Daddy. Now everybody in. Come on, Abbie."

Abbie ran down the stoop. "'Bye, Mr. Fineman!" she called, waving to the building opposite her. She couldn't resist. Mr. Fineman didn't answer, of course, but the curtains moved slightly as he stepped back from the window.

"Abbie! Abbie!" someone shouted from down the block.

Abbie stopped, halfway in the van. "Leah!" she cried. "Mom, it's Leah. I have to say good-bye one more time. Please?"

Mrs. Rosso nodded.

While Abbie was talking to Leah, Garret Klebanoff showed up to say good-bye, and Bainbridge crawled over the little kids and out of the van. Then Shirley Rosenstock showed up, and Hannah jumped out of the van. After that the Smarts and the Bermans came by, and Mr. and Mrs. Rosso got out of the van.

A half hour later, Jan and Ira were playing ball with the kids who lived in the apartment above theirs, and not a single Rosso was in the van.

Then two things happened at once. Josh Freeberg came out of the building next door, and Mrs. Rosso tapped her husband on the shoulder and said, "Honey, look at the time."

Abbie's father pulled his hand out of his pocket and

discovered that he wasn't wearing his watch. "I must have left it inside somewhere," he said. "I better go check."

"Daddy, I have to go to the bathroom," Jan announced loudly. "I'll come in with you."

Abbie blushed. Josh *would* show up just in time to hear Jan talking about the bathroom.

"Hi, Abbie," said Josh.

"Hi," Abbie replied. She glanced at Leah.

Leah grinned at Abbie and left her alone with Josh.

"I'm really going to miss you," Josh said.

"I'm going to miss you, too."

"I wish we were going to be in high school together. It would be fun."

"Yeah," said Abbie.

"If you were going to be here, I would have asked you to the first school dance."

"You would have?" Abbie couldn't believe it.

Josh nodded.

"Kids!" Mrs. Rosso called then. "Time to go!"

"I guess my dad found his watch," said Abbie. "We better say good-bye."

"Yeah. . . . Well, good-bye." Josh leaned over and brushed Abbie's cheek with his lips.

Abbie's face turned a fierce shade of red again. "'Bye, Josh," she replied, eyes to the ground.

"Whoa!" exclaimed Hannah. "Abbie and Josh, sitting in a tree, K-I-S-S-I-N-G. First comes—"

Hannah's words were cut off as Bainbridge clapped a hand over her mouth, picked her up, and carried her to the van under his arm.

"Abbie, good-bye!" cried Leah. She threw her arms around Abbie. "I'm going to miss you *so* much."

"Oh, me too," said Abbie.

"I'll write every day."

"Promise?"

Leah nodded.

"I'll write every day, too," said Abbie.

"Promise?"

Abbie nodded. "I better get going. I have to sit in the back. It's easier to get there if Bainbridge and Candy and I go in first."

"'Bye!" Leah called again.

"'Bye!" said Abbie.

When the Rossos were settled properly in the van, Abbie, Bainbridge, and Candy were in the seat farthest back. In front of them were Woody and Hardy. In front of *them* were Faustine and Dinnie, and in the first seat were Hannah, Ira, and Jan. Mr. Rosso sat in the driver's seat and Mrs. Rosso sat beside him, in the single passenger seat.

"Ready?" asked Mr. Rosso.

The Rosso kids were reflected in the rearview mirror—ten freckled faces. The freckles were one of the few things Abbie didn't like about her family. She liked having nine brothers and sisters and hoped to have ten kids herself one day. She liked the fact that the Rossos looked so much alike—brown hair, blue eyes, round faces. But she didn't like their freckles.

"Seat belts," called Mrs. Rosso.

"Daddy?" said Jan. "I have to go to the bathroom again."

"Honey, you just went," Mrs. Rosso pointed out.

"But I have to go *again*."

"I have to go too," said Ira.

"Anyone else?" asked Mrs. Rosso.

Abbie and her brothers and sisters looked at each other.

"Me," said Hardy.

"Me," said Dinnie.

"They might as well go now," said Abbie's father. "Otherwise we'll have to stop at every rest station on the New Jersey Turnpike."

Abbie looked out the window of the van. All of the neighbors, Leah and Josh included, were standing around waiting to send them off. Instead, the doors to the van opened, and Jan, Ira, Hardy, and Dinnie tumbled out, followed by Mrs. Rosso. Abbie could feel herself blushing as she shrugged at her friends.

It was ten minutes before everyone was strapped into the van again.

"Good-bye! Good-bye!" called Leah and Josh and Garret and Shirley and the Smarts and the Bermans.

"Good-bye!" called the Rossos.

The van pulled into the traffic, and Mr. Rosso edged along Thirty-first Street until he reached Park Avenue. He made a careful turn onto Park and began making his way to Forty-second Street and finally to the Lincoln Tunnel. Abbie looked long and hard at everything they passed. It was the last time she'd be looking at New York as a true New Yorker.

"Uh-oh," said Mr. Rosso, just as he was about to enter the heavy traffic feeding into the tunnel.

Eleven heads snapped to attention. The Rossos knew the sound of that "uh-oh."

Mr. Rosso was frantically patting his pockets and trying to feel inside a jacket lying on the floor of the van. "I can't find my wallet," he said grimly.

"Oh, *Ted*," Mrs. Rosso exclaimed.

"Well, we'll have to turn around," he said. "It's probably back at the house. *Every*thing's in it—credit cards, cash. I must have left it inside when I took Jan to the bathroom."

In the front seat Hannah leaned over Ira and poked Jan. "It's all *your* fault," she said.

Jan leaned over Ira and poked Hannah back. "It is not!"

"Is too!"

"Is not!"

Nobody bothered to stop the argument, and it continued as Mr. Rosso turned around and headed back to Thirty-first Street. He pulled up in front of their apartment building, and everyone except Abbie (who was too embarrassed) and Hannah and Jan (who were too cross) piled out of the van, called hello to the neighbors, and poured inside their old building to search for the wallet.

When Abbie couldn't stand the sound of her sisters' squabbling, she finally crawled up to the front seat and separated them. Jan sat down huffily on the floor next to the driver's seat. "Abbie, you are not the boss of— Hey!" she cried.

"What?" asked Hannah and Abbie.

"I found it! I found Daddy's wallet. It's right here under the seat!"

A half hour later the Rossos were back in the van, stuck in a traffic jam outside the Lincoln Tunnel. Abbie nudged Bainbridge. "I never thought I'd say this, but I can't wait to get out of New York," she told him.

"I know what you mean," he replied with a grin.

"Mommy, this is boring," said Ira from the front seat. "And the van is getting dirty. Can we close the windows?"

"Not until we're out of this traffic and we can put the air conditioning on again."

"It's *hot* today," complained Woody.

"Too hot," said Faustine. "Look at all those dogs sticking their noses out of the car windows. It's too hot for them, all right. They're panting. They're not happy."

"Poor things," said Dinnie.

All of the Rosso kids loved animals, but Faustine and Dinnie loved them the most. And they cared about *all* animals—grasshoppers and bees and spiders and turtles and cats and dogs and jungle animals and desert animals and sea animals.

"Mom, can we get a pet when we get to New Jersey?" asked Dinnie.

"Absolutely not," replied Mrs. Rosso.

"*Why* not?" asked every single Rosso kid, even though they knew what the answer would be.

"Because ten kids is enough."

That was not a fair reason, Abbie thought.

"Mom," said Hardy, "we couldn't have a pet in New York because there wasn't enough room, but now we're going to live on a *farm*."

"Yeah," agreed the others.

"But we're not going to be farmers."

"Think of all the strays we could help out," said Faustine.

"No," said Mrs. Rosso. "And that is my final word on the subject."

"Mo-om!" pleaded Dinnie.

"Dinnie, I just said no."

"Daddy, I want a pet!" said Ira.

"I have to go to the bathroom!" cried Jan.

"I'm getting carsick," moaned Hannah.

"Children, your father can't—"

*Screeeech.*

Mr. Rosso jerked on the brakes just in time to avoid hitting the car in front of them.

*"Everybody be quiet!"* roared Mr. Rosso.

"Hey! Hey! Way to go! Drive much?" called several voices to Abbie's left. She glanced out the window. A convertible full of the cutest guys in the history of the universe was next to her. The boys were pointing at the van and laughing.

Abbie slumped so far down in her seat that she was almost sitting on her neck. She wanted to die. She just wanted to *die*. Pet or no pet, New Jersey couldn't come fast enough.

# CHAPTER TWO
## *CALANDRA*

The Rossos had been living in their new house for almost two weeks. Candy thought it was just like a house in a fairy tale, but not everyone agreed with her. Mr. Rosso said it was unkempt. The stone steps leading to the back door were cracked, and moss was growing on them in spongy patches. Columbine trailed lazily up and down one side of the house. Now, in August, it looked dusty, and the leaves were a dull, faded green. By late spring, though, they would be shiny and bright again, and Candy knew from the books she read that big, colorful blooms would open. Another side of the house was overrun with Virginia creeper. Mr. Rosso said the Virginia creeper would have to go. It was destructive and choked out other plants. But Candy still thought the farmhouse was wonderful.

One hot morning in the middle of August, Candy awoke early. For a moment she lay in bed listening to the birds calling to each other. In New York she sometimes heard pigeons and sparrows. Here in the country she heard many different birds, but she couldn't identify them. She would have to ask Faustine and Dinnie about them. They knew everything about wildlife.

Candy reached over and turned on the radio as quietly as she could. She didn't want to wake Abbie, who was asleep in the other bed. (Although not much *could* wake Abbie. In New York she had slept through every single nighttime car crash that Bainbridge had kept track of.)

"Today's weather," said the radio announcer in a tinny voice, "is going to be another killer. The heat wave continues. The high is expected to reach ninety-eight. With ninety percent humidity, it's not going to be real pleasant around here, folks." But it'll be better than New York, thought Candy, even without air conditioning.

Candy switched the radio off. She pushed her sheet back and silently swung her feet to the floor. Then she tiptoed into the bathroom, where she had put her shorts and shirt and sneakers the night before. It was an old habit. In the bathroom she could dress in peace, and she didn't have to worry about waking anybody. With nine brothers and sisters you had to think of those things.

Candy crept downstairs to the kitchen, where she found her mother sitting at the table, reading the paper and sipping coffee.

"Hi, Mom," she said.

"Morning, my early bird."

Candy smiled. She liked her mother's nickname for her. And she liked being an early bird. The silent moments of the morning were her favorite part of the day.

"Is Dad gone already?" Candy asked as she poured herself a glass of orange juice.

Mrs. Rosso nodded. "He just left. He has an early meeting today."

In New York, Mr. Rosso had been able to get from the front door of the Rossos' apartment to the door of his office in twenty minutes flat. In New Jersey he left the house, was picked up by a car pool at the end of the driveway, and was driven to the train station. When he reached New York, he took a subway to his office. He arrived there two hours after he'd left the farm. It was a big adjustment for him.

Candy sat opposite her mother and opened *The Secret Garden*, which she had brought downstairs with her.

"Goodness, honey, you're almost finished with

that," said Mrs. Rosso, looking at the place Candy had opened the book to. "Didn't you just start it?"

"Mmm," replied Candy, already half-lost in the story. "Next I'm going to read *A Tree Grows in Brooklyn*. And then maybe I'll reread *The Yearling*." Candy suddenly had an idea. She looked up from the story. "Mom," she said, "if we got a pet we could name it Flag, like the deer in *The Yearling*."

"Sorry, honey. No pets. Ten—"

"I know. Ten kids is enough."

"Right."

"Today," said Candy, trying to ignore the sting of disappointment she felt, "I'm going to look for a secret garden." Candy had spent part of every day searching for a secret place. She needed one. All of her life she'd dreamed of a place where she could go and be just Candy, alone.

She wanted a spot where she could read her books and not be disturbed, where she could daydream and not be teased about it. She had never had such a place. In New York the Rosso apartment had been overrun with her brothers and sisters. Going outside was no better. As soon as she opened the door, she ran into neighbors—the Smarts or the Bermans or Shirley Rosenstock or somebody. And Mr. Fineman was *always* spying from his window.

Candy had dreamed that she'd have a room of her own in the new house, but that hadn't worked out.

The farmhouse was bigger, but it wasn't a mansion. It had five bedrooms instead of four. One was for her parents, of course. The others had been divided up among the ten children according to some system of Mrs. Rosso's that Candy hadn't quite followed. All Candy knew was that while she had *more* room, she didn't have her *own* room. She shared with Abbie. The twins had another room, and, just as in New York, the older boys—Bainbridge, Woody, and Hardy—shared the third room, and the youngest children—Hannah, Ira, and Jan—shared the fourth. The arrangement was fine, but Candy still wanted someplace private and preferably secret.

Mrs. Rosso smiled. "A secret garden? You'd probably have better luck looking for a secret place in the house."

"Really?" said Candy. "Why?"

"Just a thought. This house is over a hundred years old. And the real estate agent said something about it having once been part of the Underground Railroad."

"You mean the people who lived here hid slaves and helped them escape to Canada?"

"That's right."

"Still," said Candy, "it doesn't mean there was a secret passage or something. The slaves might have been hidden in a root cellar. Or maybe in the barn or even a chicken coop."

"True. It was just a thought."

Candy was more intrigued than she sounded. She decided to talk to Hardy that day. Hardy was an amateur detective. At least, *he* thought he was. He had shortened his name, Eberhard, to Hardy partly because his favorite detectives in the world were the Hardy Boys. Hardy wished he could be their brother, even though Woody had pointed out that then his name would be Hardy Hardy. And he had added, "Har-har. Get it? Hardy, hardy har-har?" But Hardy didn't care. Neither did Candy. So what if Hardy hadn't solved any actual cases, hadn't captured a jewel thief or tracked down a kidnapper. He *was* good at figuring things out and finding lost items. Maybe he could help her find a stop on the Underground Railroad.

"Leave me alone!"

"No, leave *me* alone! Don't touch me!"

Jan and Hannah came crashing into the kitchen. Why did they always have to be the next ones up? Candy wondered. Why couldn't Ira or the twins get up next? They were much quieter.

While her sisters messily poured out Grape Nuts, Candy ate a piece of toast and made her getaway. With her book tucked under her arm she ran down the cracked stone steps, rounded a corner of the house, and passed the tree with the twisted wisteria vine twining around its trunk. She headed off in a different direction than usual. The Rossos' house sat on fifteen acres of land, so there were plenty of places for Candy to explore.

One morning she had found the crumbling foundation of what her father thought might once have been an ice house. It had been a good spot to read—for a while. Then Woody and Hardy had found her. Another time Candy had found a tiny brook. In her excitement she had made the mistake of telling her brothers and sisters about it. Within minutes they'd all been there, shouting and wading and trying to catch minnows with their hands.

Candy walked for a long time. She walked until she wasn't sure she was on the Rossos' property anymore, but she didn't find a place that was secret or private or hidden. She leaned against an old ash tree, read until she finished *The Secret Garden*, and then decided to find Hardy. It was time to ask him for help.

Candy walked back to the house. Once, along the way, she thought she was lost, which was exciting, but soon she caught sight of the stone foundation she'd discovered several days earlier.

The house was quiet. Candy found her mother folding clothes in the laundry room. Jan was helping her. This was the clothes-folding system: Sort clothes according to owner. Separate kinds of clothes into piles—a sock pile, a T-shirt pile, and so forth. Fold each pile before going on to the next. Clothes folding that way went much faster for twelve people than you'd imagine.

"Mom, where's Hardy?" asked Candy.

"He and Woody and Ira went to the brook."

"Thanks! 'Bye!"

"I want you four back by one o'clock for lunch. If you see the others, tell them too, please."

Candy was already out the door. "Okay!" she called over her shoulder.

The sight of Ira playing in the brook was pretty interesting. Woody and Hardy were barefoot, wet, and muddy. Ira was wearing rain boots to keep his feet clean and dry. The rest of him was spotless, not a speck of mud anywhere.

"How can he catch minnows like that?" Candy whispered to Hardy after she'd been watching the boys for several moments. "How can he stay so clean?"

"I don't know," replied Hardy, "but he's caught more than me and Woody together."

"Woody and I," Candy corrected him. "Listen, Hardy." She dropped her voice. "Would you help me with something today?"

"What is it?" asked Hardy suspiciously.

Candy explained about the Underground Railroad and what the real estate agent had said.

When she was finished, Hardy let out a low whistle. "Boy, we better get right to work. Just let me change into my detective clothes."

A grin spread across Candy's face. "Great!" she exclaimed. She turned to Woody. "Hardy and I have to do something," she said. "Watch Ira, okay? And Mom says to be home by one o'clock for lunch."

"Okay," replied Woody. He and Ira were bent over a flat rock examining a large beetle. Ira examined with his eyes only; Woody poked and prodded.

When Hardy emerged from his room sometime later, he was wearing a plaid hat and carrying a magnifying glass. Candy thought he looked more like Sherlock Holmes than Frank or Joe Hardy, but she didn't tell him so. And she let him give the orders.

"Get two flashlights," he told her. "We'll start in the barn."

The barn was just one of several teetery buildings on the Rossos' property. There were also a chicken coop, a stone storage shed, and a stable. Of course, they were mostly empty, except for a lot of hay, and unused because the Rossos didn't plan to do any farming, although Mr. Rosso had stashed a few things in the storage shed.

Candy followed Hardy to the barn. "Why are we starting here?" she asked.

"It looks like the oldest building. Also, once I saw a movie where this Northern guy hid slaves in a hole he dug under his barn. He fixed it up, and the slaves could spend two or three nights in it if they needed to. Here, give me one of the flashlights and let's start looking."

"What am I looking for?"

"A secret opening or something."

Candy didn't think that was much to go on, but she began looking anyway. She and Hardy walked slowly through the barn, shining their flashlights everywhere.

"How come we're only looking on the floor?" she asked. "Maybe there was a secret place up in the loft."

"No, there wasn't," Hardy said disgustedly. "Up above? No way. Why do you think it was called the *Underground* Railroad?"

"Oh," said Candy. Maybe Hardy was a better detective than she gave him credit for.

A half hour later Candy and Hardy had found some old tools and a boot. But the floor of the barn seemed solid.

"Stable next," announced Hardy.

The stable was more interesting than the barn. Some ancient harnesses had been left behind. They hung, forgotten, in the tack room. Candy found a horseshoe in one of the stalls. She decided to hang it over her bed for good luck.

"Hey!" exclaimed Candy after she and Hardy had given the stable a thorough but disappointing once-over. "It's almost one o'clock. Lunchtime."

By the time lunch was over, Hardy the detective had lost all interest in detecting. Woody wanted him to play skydivers in the barn loft, and that sounded much more appealing to him.

"*Sky*divers?" Mrs. Rosso repeated.

"It's safe, Mom. Honest."

Bainbridge snorted. "Look who's talking. The king of the emergency room."

Woody bristled immediately. "I am *not* the king of the emergency room."

"Oh, sure," said Hannah. "Broken wrist, broken thumb, three broken toes, concussion, stitches in your forehead—"

"All right, all right, all right. But Mom," Woody went on, "this game is safe. All we do is jump into the hay in the loft."

"Jump from *where*, Mr. Daredevil? Bainbridge, Abbie, go with them and use your heads about things. But not literally, okay?"

"Sure," they replied, grinning.

Candy watched her detective run out the back door with Woody, Bainbridge, and Abbie, followed by Ira and Jan. She sighed loudly.

"Honey, would you put the folded clothes away, please?" asked Mrs. Rosso. "They're stacked in the laundry room."

Candy went straight to the laundry room. She wouldn't have disobeyed her mother, but it wasn't as if she had anything better to do.

She had to make four trips before she'd lugged all of the clean laundry upstairs. According to Mrs. Rosso's clothes distribution system, Candy placed everything on her mother and father's big bed and grouped the piles by bedroom. Then she carried the boys' clothes to their room, the little kids' clothes to their room, and so forth. The sheets and towels were last. Candy opened the big cedar linen closet. Shelves ran up and down both sides. She stacked the flat sheets, the fitted sheets, the pillow cases, and the towels neatly on the shelves.

When she was finished, she stepped as far into the closet as she could and leaned against the back wall, inhaling deeply. Cedar was one of her favorite smells in—

*Thud!* Candy suddenly stumbled backward.

*Backward!* thought Candy with alarm as she fell. I was leaning against the wall. How could I fall backward?

Candy looked around. In front of her was the linen closet with its piles of sheets. But she was in another room, a room she'd never seen before.

"A secret place in my own house!" whispered Candy. "It must be Narnia. I walked through a closet and into another world, just like Susan did in *The*

*Lion, the Witch and the Wardrobe.*"

Of course, Candy wasn't in another world, but she *was* in a hidden room. She stepped cautiously back into the closet. "Hey, you gu—" she started to shout. But she stopped. She couldn't tell anyone what she'd found or the room wouldn't be just hers anymore.

She went back into the little room and pushed the door to the closet until it was almost, but not quite, closed. Then she examined her new surroundings. The room was in the shape of a lopsided rectangle, and it was very small. The only light that came in was from a small round window, which Candy had noticed from the outside of the farmhouse but hadn't been able to find inside. The walls were wooden and rough, not plastered like those in the rest of the house, and everything was dusty, dusty, dusty.

Two pieces of furniture, both ancient-looking, occupied the room—a tall, skinny table with a drawer under the top and a straight-as-an-arrow wooden chair. Candy tried to peer out the window, but it was too dirty. She'd have to come back and clean it. Then she cautiously opened the drawer in the table. A small red leather book lay inside. On the cover, in gold letters, she read "Diary."

Candy drew in her breath. This was better than anything she'd ever read about in a story. She removed the diary, sat down in the uncomfortable chair, and opened the cover of the little book. In careless handwriting in faded blue ink were the words "Celia McIntyre, age 12."

My age, thought Candy.

Not feeling the slightest bit guilty, she read the first page. It was dated January 1, 1901. "I have a secret room," it began, "and now I have a secret diary to write in."

Candy was intrigued. She settled back in the chair and became lost in Celia's life.

From what Candy could gather, the McIntyres had lived in the farmhouse at the turn of the century. Celia was the youngest of four children, and her two older brothers and older sister were already married. In fact, Celia had a nephew who was older than she was.

Celia seemed to be a con artist. She could get almost anything from anyone, especially her parents. She had her own pony to ride and a fabulous dollhouse and was very proud of something she'd been given for Christmas called a fur muff. The one thing Celia's parents would not let her have, no matter how much she begged, was a pet in the house. The McIntyres were a farm family and had plenty of outdoor animals, but Mrs. McIntyre put her foot down when Celia suggested a house pet.

"I want only one teeny little pet," Celia wrote, "but Mother says no."

Candy could picture her pouting and knew just

how Celia felt: angry and maybe a little lonely. It was amazing how much Celia and Candy had in common. The truth was, despite her nine brothers and sisters, Candy sometimes felt lonely. She liked being alone, but at times she felt an emptiness that she was sure only a pet could fill. And she thought it was very unfair and selfish of her mother to say no to any pet at all.

When Candy got tired of reading about everything Celia wanted, she skipped ahead. She turned randomly to April tenth—and gasped. Celia's best friend had been given a parakeet, which she wasn't allowed to have, so she secretly gave it to Celia, who secretly put it in the little room and kept it there, hidden from her parents.

"Wow," said Candy out loud. "Someone hid a *pet* here once!"

Candy sat in the room for over an hour, reading Celia's diary. At last, with a sigh, she returned it to the drawer in the table. Then she walked back into the cedar closet. She didn't want anyone to get suspicious about where she'd been.

Candy smiled and hugged the wonderful secret of the room to herself. At last she had a place where she could go to be just Candy, alone.

# CHAPTER THREE
## *IRA*

"You hid it!"

"I did not. You just lost it! You're always losing things."

"I am not!"

"Are too!"

"Am not!"

Ira awoke slowly. He awoke to the sound of his sisters quarreling. He buried his head under his pillow and tried to drown out the sound of their voices. But Jan and Hannah were very loud.

Ira felt someone tweak his toes. "Get up, you lazybones. It's the first day of school!" exclaimed Hannah.

Ira sat up in a flash. The first day of school. How could he have forgotten? The summer was over.

Today was the first day of second grade, and Ira
would go to a new school, with new classmates, and
have a new teacher. His teacher's name was Miss
Price, and she was in charge of Room 2C. Ira had met
her the day before when his mother had taken all of
the Rossos to their new schools to register.

Ira's stomach felt funny, not good at all. He remembered that it had felt that way the morning they
were going to move, and his father had told him that
his stomach had butterflies in it.

Ira rolled out of bed and stuck his feet into his slippers. He had left them by his bed the night before.
Then he pulled up the covers and tucked them under
the mattress. It never took Ira long to make his bed.
His big sister Abbie had once said, "It's amazing. Ira
even *sleeps* neatly."

Ira couldn't help it. Neat was the way he was. And
he couldn't help the way his family was either. He
couldn't help that he had nine brothers and sisters or
that some of them had names like Dagwood or Gardenia. Those things were just part of his mother's systems. But Ira was worried. All those things that he
couldn't help were bound to be discovered by his
classmates, and then Ira would be teased. He was too
neat, and the Rossos were too weird and too many.

After breakfast that morning, Mrs. Rosso handed
out ten lunches in alphabetical order: Abbie, Bainbridge, Candy, Dagwood, Eberhard, Faustine, Gar-

denia, Hannah, Ira, and Jan. Then she shooed the kids out the front door in alphabetical order. The Rossos ran to the end of their driveway, knapsacks and bookbags and lunch boxes bumping along. They didn't want to be late for their buses.

Ira watched the high school bus come by and pick up Abbie. He felt sorry for her. As he waved to her through the window, he suddenly thought that his big sister looked . . . little. Then he watched the middle school bus roll to a stop and swallow up Bainbridge, Candy, and Woody. Finally, the elementary school bus, the Bluebird, stopped for Hardy, the twins, Hannah, Ira, and Jan. A Rosso for every grade except kindergarten.

"Come on, Jan, sit with me," said Ira helpfully.

Jan was the littlest Rosso, and Ira felt it was his duty to look out for her.

The Rossos' arrival didn't go unnoticed.

"Hey, just one family, and they make a whole bus stop!" a boy called.

Ira turned around, bristling, but saw Hardy and Hannah in the seat behind him. "Don't say anything," Hardy murmured without moving his lips. Ira knew Hardy was mad about what the kid had said and also mad that he had to sit with his sister.

Ira glanced at the twins, in front of him. They weren't paying attention. They were talking together in their own secret twin language.

Which was another thing. Wait till the kids heard Faustine and Dinnie's funny words. Adults thought the twins' private language was cute. Kids thought it was weird.

Ira ignored the other bus riders until the Bluebird pulled up in front of John Bowen Elementary. Then he took Jan's hand, led her to the front of the bus, and jumped down the steps with her to the sidewalk. The twins were already there. Hannah and Hardy followed Ira and Jan.

"Do you guys know where you're going?" asked Hardy gruffly. He wanted to separate himself from the rest of the Rossos.

"Yes," said the twins and added privately, "Getchup." They giggled.

"Yes," said Hannah, standing alone.

"Yes," said Ira.

"No," said Jan.

"Don't worry, Jan. I'll take you," Ira told her gallantly. He looked around. He'd never imagined that a school could sit out in the middle of cornfields and trees. John Bowen Elementary looked lost and lonely. It needed other buildings around it—skyscrapers and apartment houses and maybe a delicatessen or a candy stand.

The twins and Hardy and Hannah walked off.

"Come on, Jan," said Ira.

Ira took his sister to Room 1B and left her with Mr.

Heppler. Jan looked like she was going to cry, and Ira wanted to stay with her and help her put her things in her cubby, but Mr. Heppler showed him to the door.

"I'm right across the hall!" Ira called to Jan as he spotted the pumpkin on the door of 2C.

The butterflies in Ira's stomach were flapping around wildly. Ira stepped through the doorway. There was Miss Price, writing something on the blackboard.

"Good morning, Ira," she said warmly. "Let me show you your desk."

Miss Price led Ira to a desk in the front row. "This is yours," she said. "And over here is your cubby. You can hang your sweater on the hook, and keep anything here that you don't put in your desk, okay?"

Ira nodded. He took off his sweater and hung it up. Then he placed his lunch box on the floor of the cubby. He put his pencil case inside his desk. There. He was ready for second grade.

Ira sat at his desk. He folded his hands. He watched the other children arrive. Some of them looked at Ira, but none of them said anything. So far, so good. Maybe if Ira didn't say anything either, his classmates would never find out that he had nine brothers and sisters.

"Good morning, boys and girls!" said Miss Price. She was standing in front of the blackboard. Ira's classmates stopped talking and running around. They slid into the chairs behind the desks.

"My name is Miss Price," the teacher continued. She wrote "Miss Price" on the board. "Now you know *my* name," she said, "but I don't know all of yours. You can help me by raising your hand and saying 'here' when I call your name."

Miss Price began to call the roll: Andy Asher, Erica Cashman, Cindy Dunham. Ira could tell she was reading the names in alphabetical order. Ira knew a lot about alphabetical order.

"Roger Pratt."

"Here!"

"Jean Reston."

"Here!"

"Ira Rosso."

Ira raised his hand. "Here!"

Miss Price paused. "Class, Ira is our new student," she said. "He's just moved here. And there's something very interesting about his family. Ira has *nine* brothers and sisters." Miss Price sounded impressed.

Even though Ira continued to look straight at Miss Price, he could feel every one of his classmates staring at him. His face grew warm. But he didn't move a muscle.

How could Miss Price do such a terrible thing to him? Ira had barely opened his mouth, and the secret was out anyway. Darn that old Miss Price. Ira wanted to hate her, but hating your teacher was not a very good way to start second grade. Ira decided to give her one more chance. But *only* one more.

Miss Price finished calling the roll. Then she handed out some books—spellers and readers and arithmetic workbooks. All morning Ira paid careful attention to Miss Price. He listened to her and followed her instructions. At snacktime nobody said a word to him. Ira sat by himself and ate his peach. Maybe John Bowen Elementary wouldn't be so bad after all. And so far Miss Price hadn't blown her second chance.

When it was time for lunch, Ira lined up and walked single file with his class to the cafeteria. He sat at the end of Miss Price's table. His classmates talked and giggled and swapped the food in their lunch boxes. When the recess bell rang, Ira followed the others outside. The second-graders had recess with the third-graders. Ira stood on tiptoe and looked for Hannah.

"Hey, kid! Ira?"

Ira turned around. It was Roger Pratt from his class. "Hi," said Ira.

"Do you really have nine brothers and sisters?"

Ira nodded.

A few kids joined Roger. Ira didn't recognize all of them.

"How come?" asked Jean Reston.

Ira shrugged.

"Do you all go to John Bowen?" Roger wanted to know.

"Nope," replied Ira. "Only six of us do."

A tall boy in the back of the crowd started to laugh. "My friend says there's a new kid in his class named Eberhard Rosso. He must be your brother."

"Eberhard!" hooted a couple of girls.

"In my sister's class," said Jean, "there are two girls—twins—named Faustine and Gardenia. Faustine and Gardenia *Rosso.*"

"So?" said Ira fiercely.

"So those are the weirdest names we've ever heard," said Roger.

"*And,*" continued Jean, "I heard this new girl say she's even got two brothers named Bainbridge and Dagwood."

The kids laughed harder. Roger fell onto the black-top and rolled back and forth, clutching his stomach.

Leave it to Hannah, thought Ira. Hannah and her big mouth. She must have told about Bainbridge and Dagwood.

"You know who Dagwood is?" said Roger, still laughing. "He's a goofy cartoon character. I saw him in an old comic. Dagwood Bumstead. And he ate big sandwiches called Dagwoods!"

"Dagwoods!"

"Dagwood Bumstead!"

All of the kids were laughing. But they weren't

paying attention to Ira. They were watching Roger. Ira crept away and sat on the bottom rung of the monkey bars. He decided to stay there until the bell rang and recess was over. He didn't even get up when Roger called to him, "Hey, kid! Want to play kickball?"

"No," Ira replied. "The field's too muddy. . . . And my name's not 'kid.' It's Ira."

Ira watched Roger put his arm across Andy Asher's shoulders. The two of them walked away laughing, their heads bent together.

Back in Miss Price's room, Ira tried to forget about Roger and Andy and Jean and the tall boy. He fixed his eyes straight ahead and listened to his teacher.

"Class," she said, "it's time for sharing hour. Every afternoon after recess, you'll have a chance to share something special or important with the class. Does anyone have anything to share today?"

Ira listened to Erica Cashman talk about her kitten. The class seemed very impressed. Then he listened to Cindy Dunham telling about the new cow on her dairy farm and Andy telling about the Laser Tag game he had gotten for his birthday. The other kids oohed and aahed.

Ira got an idea.

"Does anyone else have something to share?" asked Miss Price.

Ira waved his hand.

Miss Price looked a little surprised. "Yes, Ira?" she said. "Come on up to the front of the room."

Ira stood up. He could hear a few kids snickering. He heard somebody say something about ten kids.

"Well," said Ira, "I want to tell you about all the animals on our farm. We don't have just pigs and cows and stuff. We have two ferrets and a boa constrictor—"

"Ew," said Jean.

"—and a monkey. That's why we moved to the farm. There wasn't room for any animals in our apartment in New York. So Daddy said, 'I guess we'll just have to get a farm. Then you can have all the animals you want.' And we found a hurt bobcat, so we're keeping it till it gets well, and we have a parrot, and we're going to get a lion cub—"

"Ira," Miss Price broke in, "are you *sure* about that?"

Ira nodded. "Yes. My father works for an advertising company and sometimes they make commercials for TV, and they used this lion cub in a commercial. But it doesn't have a home, so we're going to take it. We've got lots and lots of room on our farm."

"Wow!" exclaimed Roger. "Do you really have a boa constrictor?"

"Yup," said Ira. "And a tarantula."

"How big is the bobcat?" asked Jean.

"It's not full grown," Ira replied. "It's about this big." He held his hands apart.

"What does the snake eat?" asked Andy.

"Mice," said Ira. "We have a whole cage full of them."

The classroom was buzzing. The kids could barely pay attention to Miss Price that afternoon. As soon as the bell rang at the end of the day, Ira's classmates crowded around him.

"Has the tarantula ever bitten you?" asked a boy whose name Ira couldn't remember.

"What would you do if the snake got loose?" asked Jean.

Ira and the kids walked into the hall together. Ira smiled. Friends at last.


The next day during sharing hour Jean Reston raised her hand. "I don't have anything to share," she said. "I just want to ask if Ira can bring some of his pets to school."

"I'll have to ask my mom," replied Ira.

On Monday, Jean repeated her request.

"My mom said no," Ira told the class.

On Tuesday, Andy raised his hand. "I want Ira to bring in a picture of his tarantula. And also of his boa constrictor eating a mouse."

"Our camera's broken," said Ira. He saw Andy and

Roger look at each other and roll their eyes.

On Wednesday, Roger announced, "Guess what. My mom said any time it's okay with Ira's mom, I can go over to his house to see the animals. So Ira, just ask your mother and tell me what she says."

Ira felt a knot in his stomach. "Okay," he said in a small voice.

Ira didn't sleep very well that night. What was he supposed to tell Roger? That his mother had said he could *never* invite a friend over? That didn't sound very nice—or very likely.

Ira lay in his bed with the covers kicked back. He listened to the gentle sleeping sounds of Jan and Hannah. Another thought occurred to him. He did, after all, have nine brothers and sisters. One of them was bound to have a friend over who was bound to say that there wasn't a single animal on the Rosso farm. Not even a chicken or a cow, let alone a tarantula or a bobcat. There was only one thing to do, Ira decided, and he would do it right away.

Ira tiptoed out of his room and listened for sounds that would tell him where his parents were. After a moment he heard the TV and knew they were downstairs in the living room watching the news. When Ira had been little—four or five years old, he used to wonder what his parents did after he and his brothers and sisters went to sleep each night. Now that he was seven, he knew. They only did two things. They watched the news on TV, then they went to bed. Pretty boring.

"Mom?" said Ira, pausing in the doorway to the living room.

Mrs. Rosso looked up, concerned. "Ira? Are you sick, honey?"

"No," he replied, and then he burst into tears.

Mr. Rosso turned off the TV set, and Ira told his parents everything about Miss Price and his class-mates and the animal stories. "I just wanted the kids to like me," he finished up.

"And now they want to see the animals," Mr. Rosso said thoughtfully.

Ira nodded. He was cuddled up between his parents on the couch, but he felt miserable. "I want Roger to come over, but he'll find out we don't have a tarantula or a snake or a bobcat."

The Rossos were quiet for several moments. At last Mrs. Rosso said, "Would you like me to talk to Miss Price for you, honey?"

Ira heaved a great sigh. "Yes, please," he replied.

"All right. I'll call her after school tomorrow."

On Thursday, Mrs. Rosso made her call, and on Friday, Ira jumped off the school bus and ran to Miss Price's room so he could be the first one there. Miss Price was waiting for him.

"Hi," said Ira sheepishly.

"Hi, Ira," Miss Price answered. "I spoke to your mother."

"I know. Are you mad?"

Miss Price smiled. "Maybe I'm a little bit mad at the stories you told, but I'm not mad at you. Do you understand, though? No more storytelling?"

"Never," said Ira.

"Now," Miss Price went on, "we have to straighten things out with the other kids. And I think the only thing to do is tell them the truth."

Ira swallowed hard. "Mom told me about that, too. I don't want to do it."

"It may not be as bad as you think. I'd like you to try it during sharing time today. Then you can tell the whole class. You'll only have to say it once."

"Okay," Ira finally agreed reluctantly, but his knees felt like water.

At sharing time that day Duncan Fox told how his dog Jupiter was learning fancy tricks like the dogs on TV could do. April Ingram said that her parents were taking her to Disney World for her birthday. When April was finished, Miss Price turned to Ira. "Don't you have something you'd like to share?" she said.

Ira's cheeks burned bright pink. He stood up very slowly. "Yes," he replied.

The class started to whisper. Ira could hear the kids saying things like "another new animal" and "maybe the lion cub came."

Ira faced his classmates. "Um," he said, "I want to say that I—I don't have any animals." Ira glanced at Miss Price, who nodded at him encouragingly, but his tongue felt like it was glued into his mouth with peanut butter. "I made that up," he continued. "There are no animals at all on our farm. Not even regular farm animals."

"*What?*" someone exclaimed.

Ira felt tears coming to his eyes, but he told himself not to cry. Crying would be worse than all the stories he had told. He drew in a deep, shaky breath.

"My mom won't let us get a pet. She says ten kids is enough.... I'm sorry. I just wanted ... just wanted"—Ira's voice was dropping—"you to like me," he finished in a whisper. He dropped into his seat and buried his head in his arms.

For a moment the class was silent. Ira waited for the laughter to start. Instead, Duncan Fox raised his hand.

"Yes, Duncan?" said Miss Price.

"Jupiter isn't really learning any TV tricks," he said. "I just made that up because Ira always has such good things to share."

Ira dared to look up.

Andy Asher raised his hand. "Well, I really do have Laser Tag," he said, "but my mom and dad gave it to me because they won't get me a pet either. I want Ira to come over and play sometime. I don't care if he has animals or not."

Ira beamed. The knot in his stomach disappeared. *"Sure,"* he replied. And when school was over that afternoon, he invited both Roger and Andy to his house to go wading in the brook. "We really do have a brook," he added. "Honest."

# CHAPTER FOUR
## *DAGWOOD*

Green slime, Woody was thinking. Monster warts, toadstool juice, Dracula's fangs. . . . What a waste.

Dagwood Rosso stood in Zinder's Dime Store. He was surrounded by makeup and mustaches, warts and wigs, capes and costumes. It was almost Halloween, Woody's favorite time of year.

"But what a *waste*," he said out loud. "All this great stuff and no reason to wear it."

"Isn't your homeroom having a party in school?" asked Hardy, fingering a little bottle of fake blood.

"Yeah, but big deal," replied Woody. "So someone's mother brings in cupcakes or something. That's kid stuff. I want to go trick-or-treating the way we used to in New York. Hey, maybe we could go back to

New York for Halloween."

"Don't count on it," said Bainbridge, coming up behind his brothers.

"I'll say," added Abbie.

Woody scowled. What a gyp. In New York, where the Rossos knew most of their neighbors, all they had to do was go to each apartment building on their block, and they ended up with a whole bag of candy. That's how many people lived nearby. But here in New Jersey they couldn't even see their closest neighbors from their house. We could walk twenty miles and come back with three Hershey bars, thought Woody crossly.

He wished his mother would hurry up and finish her shopping so the Rossos could go home and he wouldn't have to torture himself anymore by looking at the costumes. He wandered to the front of the store and stood by the doorway, watching the sidewalk outside so he'd be sure to see his mother the moment she appeared.

"What's wrong with you?" asked Hannah. "Didn't you find a costume?" Hannah was standing at the cash register, paying for a wart and a pair of green rubber hands. Every year she dressed up as a witch, and every year her costume got a little better.

"There's no point," replied Woody. "We can't go trick-or-treating, and in middle school you don't dress up for class parties. There's not enough time." Woody didn't know whether that was true. He had just made it up. But it sounded good.

"Gosh," said Hannah, serious for once. "That's awful. You mean in three years there won't be any point to my witch costume?" She paused. Then she blurted out, "Well, why don't we ask Mom if *we* can give a Halloween party?"

"Huh?"

"A party. For our friends. At our house. We can have prizes for costumes, and we'll play games and give out candy. It won't be like trick-or-treating, but it would be fun. Quick, get everyone to agree before Mom comes."

"Okay," replied Woody, feeling slightly awed. A Halloween party really could be fun. It wouldn't be like trick-or-treating, but it would be a whole lot better than just sitting at his desk eating a cupcake with a pumpkin face on it. Woody began to think of all the things they could do at a Halloween party. His heart began to beat faster. He ran off in search of the other kids.

Woody found Jan in the toy department looking at a stuffed cat.

"Will you buy this for me, Woody?" she begged.

"Can't," he replied. "Where's Ira?"

"Over there." Jan pointed to the candy counter.

"Come on. We have to round everyone up."

"Why?"

"You'll see." Woody grabbed his sister by the wrist, got Ira by the other wrist, and led them back to the aisle where the Halloween supplies were displayed. Hannah had found Faustine, Gardenia, and Candy. And Hardy, Abbie, and Bainbridge were right where Woody had left them.

"What's going on?" asked Abbie.

"I've got an idea," said Hannah. "Let's ask Mom if we can have a Halloween party at our house. Wouldn't that be great? We can't go trick-or-treating, and Halloween's on a Friday this year . . . isn't it? Think of all the stuff we could do."

"You mean like bob for apples?" asked Dinnie.

Her twin nudged her. "Globark."

Dinnie nudged her back, shaking her head. "En cad sam."

They looked at each other seriously, identical freckled faces.

Dagwood frowned. He never knew what to make of the twins.

"Anyway," Hannah continued, "we could give out prizes for costumes."

"We could have a fortune-teller!" exclaimed Candy. "We'll make Mom dress up in a turban and lots of jewelry!"

"Yeah!" agreed the others.

"Will there be candy?" asked Jan.

"Sure," replied Hannah.

It was at that point in the conversation that Woody had a great idea. He didn't know where it had come from, but it was one of the best ideas of his life. "You guys," he said slowly. "You know what? We could make a spook house in the basement. Hang cobwebs from the ceiling, rig up ghosts, make the kids touch peeled grapes and tell them they're eyeballs—"

"Woody, you're a genius!" Abbie exclaimed. "Boy, this is going to be the best Halloween ever!"

"You think so?" Woody replied.

"I hope so," she said.

"Hey, everybody," Bainbridge spoke up, "get ready. Here comes Mom."

The Rossos took their cue from their biggest brother. He knew what to do in any situation. They could count on him for that. Bainbridge pretended to be examining an eyepatch with great interest. The others turned back to the display.

Woody found that he didn't have to pretend to be interested in the costumes. If they were going to have a party, then he'd need one after all, and he wanted it to be really great.

He wanted to be Kromar the Magnificent, the World's Most Dazzling Magician.

"Hi, kids," said Mrs. Rosso.

"Oh, Mom," Bainbridge replied. "Are you done already? We didn't know you were here."

"I'm done. Have you all finished your shopping?"

"Yes," replied Bainbridge, sounding dejected. "We didn't buy much. Didn't see the point."

Woody caught on immediately. "I'm not buying anything," he announced. "I won't be needing a costume this year."

"But Woody!" Mrs. Rosso looked concerned. "You love Halloween."

"I know." Woody hung his head. "We can't go trick-or-treating, though. Our neighbors are too spread out. And in school we're just going to have a dumb old class party."

"It's too bad there's not even a school party—a big one—that kids of all ages could go to," added Abbie.

"It *is* too bad," Mrs. Rosso agreed, shepherding her children out of the store.

"Hey!" said Bainbridge, as if an idea had just occurred to him. "Maybe we could have our own party. . . . Nah."

"What do you mean 'nah'?" said Mrs. Rosso. "Bainbridge, that's a great idea. It would help you get to know some more kids. If each of you invited two friends, let's see, that would be thirty people. . . ." Mrs. Rosso was standing by the door to the van, gazing above her, lost in thought.

Woody turned to Bainbridge and secretly, excitedly, gave him the thumbs-up sign. Bainbridge grinned back.

By that evening it was settled. Mrs. Rosso had mentioned the party to Mr. Rosso, who of course had agreed to the idea. Actually, Woody wasn't sure his father had heard the question. He'd been poring over his plans for the wall unit he was finally going to build. Mrs. Rosso had made several valiant attempts to capture his attention and had finally given up.

"So a party with thirty children is all right with you?" she had asked.

"Mmm."

Mrs. Rosso took that as a yes.

Woody was beside himself with excitement. "Kromar the Magnificent," he told Hardy. "That's who I'm going to be. We'll have to make another trip to Zinder's. I need that top hat I saw there, and a wand —maybe one of those wands that collapses when you hand it to some— Hey! Hey! Oh, wow! I just had another great idea!"

"What?" asked Hardy.

"Jan! She hasn't made up her mind about a costume. She never knows what she wants to be. I'll ask her to dress up as my assistant! She can wear, oh, one of those leotard things. . . ."

Woody's mind was racing. Halloween was only three weeks away. There was so much to do.

Over the next two weeks, piece by piece, Woody put together his Kromar costume. There was a box of old clothes, mostly bits and pieces of past Halloween costumes, in the attic of the Rossos' new house. In it Woody found a cape, a black cummerbund, and a snappy black bow tie. If he put them on with his white dress shirt, black dress pants, and shiny black dress shoes, he'd look dashing and mysterious. At Zinder's he did buy the hat and a collapsible wand, as well as a red paper carnation to pin to his shirt.

Jan agreed to be his assistant. It solved the problem of what costume to choose, and she liked the idea of dressing up in something sparkly. Mrs. Rosso found an old leotard and sewed sequins all over it. Then Woody and Jan glued glitter to a pair of tights. Furthermore, Jan got to wear her black patent-leather party shoes, something she always looked forward to with great anticipation.

So Woody was set—sort of. "I just have the feeling I'm missing something," he told Hardy one night.

Hardy looked up from the Hardy Boys mystery he was reading. "Missing something?" Missing items were of great interest to him. "What is it? I bet I can find it for you."

"No, you can't," Woody told him, "because I don't know what it is I'm missing. My costume just needs something more, that's all. It's a good costume, but . . . I think I need a prop."

"You've got a prop," said Hardy. "You've got two. You've got the wand and Jan."

"I know, I know." Woody frowned. He was sure he was missing something.

His problem was solved in school the next day.

When Woody entered his homeroom, the first thing he saw, propped on a desk in the second row, was a sign painted on white oaktag: Free Rabbits, it said. Sign Up Now. At the bottom was a picture of a pink-eyed, cotton-tailed bunny.

A rabbit! Woody thought. Perfect.

Woody approached the desk. "Hi, Bart," he said to the boy behind the sign.

"Hi, Woody." Bart peered at Woody through glasses as thick as the petrie dishes they used in science class.

"You've got rabbits?" asked Woody.

"Yup," replied Bart. "Fluffer-Nut just had another litter. She keeps having them. My mom says I either have to find homes for all the babies or get rid of Fluffer-Nut."

"Whoa," said Woody slowly.

"You want one?" asked Bart hopefully.

"Well . . . I was wondering if I could just borrow one."

"You want to *borrow* a baby rabbit?"

"Only for one night."

"But I have to give these rabbits *away*. I don't want them back. How come you want to borrow one?"

"Because my mom won't let us have a pet. But on Halloween my brothers and sisters and I are going to have a party, and I'm going to be Kromar the Magnificent, a magician. And a magician needs a rabbit to pull out of his hat. By the way, you're invited to the party." Woody hadn't intended to ask Bart to the party, but Bart was nice enough, and Woody knew him as well as he knew any of the other boys in his class. He also knew that serious, bespectacled Bart (who tended to spit when he said his *s*'s) wasn't very popular and would probably be thrilled with the invitation—and therefore more apt to lend Fluffer-Nut's baby to him.

"*I'm* invited?" Bart repeated, his voice rising to a squeak.

"Sure," replied Woody generously. "So can I borrow one of Fluffer-Nut's babies?"

"I guess so," said Bart. "I'll bring one with me when I come to the party."

So it was settled. Woody was confident that he'd have one of the best costumes at the party. Furthermore, he would have a pet for one night.

On Halloween afternoon every single Rosso made a beeline for the school buses, and as soon as they were dropped off, ran up the long driveway to the farm-house. Woody, Candy, and Bainbridge were the last to arrive. As the middle-school bus drove off and they dashed to the house, Woody noticed two maple trees, each with only half of its yellow leaves left, silhou-etted against the darkening sky. The smell of hickory smoke was in the air, and since the temperature had been dropping steadily all day, Woody could see his breath for the first time that fall. The moon was going to be full that night. It hung palely in the sky now but later would turn an orange almost as brilliant as the pumpkin sitting on the front porch.

"We're here!" cried Woody as they crashed through the door and tossed their things in the back hall.

"Great," said Mrs. Rosso, looking up from a plate of sandwiches she was fixing. "There are all sorts of things to be done. Abbie and the twins are decorating the family room. I need someone to help me with the food, Jan needs someone to help her with her cos-tume, and Woody, you better get to work in the base-ment. . . ."

"Sure," replied Woody, but first he wandered through the house just looking around. He felt more excited with every step he took. A grinning jack-o'-lantern sat in the hallway by the front door. Someone had suspended several paper bats from the ceiling. In the family room orange and black crepe paper was strung from side to side and corner to corner, and a bunch of orange and black balloons was tied in the very middle of the room.

Woody finally went to the basement but not until after he had recruited Bainbridge, Hardy, and Hannah to help him with the spookhouse. Following Woody's eager directions, they wound a rope from pole to pole, from dryer to work table, forming a "walk" to follow through the darkened room. Woody had worked hard planning the spookhouse. It would be lit only by flashlights shining through gruesome masks. The guests would feel cobwebs on their faces, hear the "haunted house" track from Woody's sound effects tape, and generally be scared silly.

By six thirty, everything was ready. The food had been set out, Woody and his brothers and sisters were wearing their costumes, and Mr. Rosso, who had left the city early, was sitting behind a wooden stand in the family room, a turban wrapped around his head. He was Madame Zilva, the fortune-teller. (Mrs. Rosso had turned down the job offer.)

Twenty guests had been invited to the party, and by seven fifteen they had all arrived. Bart showed up with a small white bunny, as he had promised, and Woody dropped the rabbit into his hat and strutted around with Jan all evening. Sometimes he would flap his cape about him, laugh mysteriously, and cry, "I am Kromar the Magnificent!"

Madame Zilva was a big hit. Woody had his fortune told twice. The first time, his father said, "I see that you have recently moved to a farm. . . . In your future I see seventh grade. In your past I see fifth grade."

"Da-ad," Woody complained.

The second time, his father said, "I see someone healthy, wealthy, and wise in your future. . . . Yes, you are going to marry Benjamin Franklin."

Woody laughed and gave up. He escorted Jan through the spookhouse. "Ew!" she kept exclaiming. "Yuck!"

The evening sped by. Food was eaten, apples were bobbed for, a neighbor from miles away was invited over to be an impartial judge of the costumes. Woody was awarded a wind-up Frankenstein for Most Realistic Costume.

At nine thirty parents began arriving to take the guests home.

"Guess what?" Bart said to Woody when he saw his mother at the door. "I can't take the rabbit home with me. Fluffer-Nut is going to have more babies. I had to tell Mom I was *giving* you the rabbit."

"Oh, yeah?" replied Woody. Hmm, he thought. Instead of panicking he said, "Don't worry about it. I'll figure something out."

Woody put the rabbit in a box, put the box in his bedroom, and closed the door. Then he helped his family clean up. With twelve pairs of hands at work, and Mrs. Rosso's clean-up system in full swing, the house was quickly back to normal except for a few decorations that Jan insisted on leaving up.

As soon as Woody and his brothers were in their bedroom, Woody opened the box and showed them Fluffer-Nut's baby.

"Why is it still here?" asked Bainbridge sternly.

"Because Bart's mother won't let Bart take it back. Fluffer-Nut is going to have babies again."

"Well, what do you think *you're* going to do with it?"

"Keep it." Woody grinned. "It's homeless now. Don't you think Mom will feel sorry for it?"

"Not on your life," said Abbie's voice. She poked her head into the room. "She'll find a way to give it back. She'll see right through us. She doesn't fall for *any*thing where a pet is concerned. I just don't understand her. She is so selfish about pets. It's not as if one of us was allergic or something."

"Yeah," agreed Candy, appearing behind her sister in the doorway. "Boy, is Mom unreasonable."

"Who else is out there?" asked Woody.

"All of us," said Abbie.

"You guys better come in and close the door," said Bainbridge.

The kids crowded into the boys' room.

"Well," said Woody. "I finally got us a pet."

"But," said Bainbridge, "what are we going to do with it?"

Silence.

Finally Candy spoke up. "I know a place where we can hide it." She heaved a great sigh, hating to give up her one and only spot for privacy, but it was worth it for a pet. "I found a secret room. Come on. I'll show you."

Nobody really believed Candy, so they followed her amid groans and comments such as "Oh, *sure*" and "Yeah, right." But when Candy pushed open the back of the linen closet, the comments changed to "I don't believe it!" and "Why didn't you show us before?"

Candy told them the whole story about wanting a private place and discovering the room. She even showed them Celia's diary. "See, Woody?" she said. "Celia hid a pet in here once. We can hide the rabbit. We'll have a pet, and Mom and Dad won't even know."

"Yeah . . ." said Woody slowly.

"Abbie?" asked Candy, turning to her older sister for permission.

Eighteen eyes fixed their gazes on Abbie.

"I guess we can try it," she said. "But remember, this is a *secret*, everybody. It's the only way we'll get to have a pet. Okay, Jan?"

Jan was very poor at keeping secrets, but she nodded her head solemnly.

So the rabbit was named Secret and hidden in the dark, musty room. Woody fixed up a cage for him, and he and the other Rosso kids took turns bringing him fresh water and carrots and lettuce.

After three days Jan said, "He never hops around anymore."

After four days Hannah complained, "All he does is sleep."

It was the twins who were able to speak the truth. "He's depressed," they said. "We can't keep him cooped up in this room. He needs sunshine and fresh air. He needs to hop around outside."

Woody nodded unhappily. The twins were right. They knew everything about animals. Besides, anyone could see that Secret was miserable.

"All right. That does it," exclaimed Woody. "I'm going to talk to Mom."

"*What?*" screeched Hannah.

"Keep your voice down," Woody hissed. He faced Hannah and the twins, who were with him in the hidden room. "Do you want Mom to discover this place?"

"Well, how are you going to talk to her about Secret without telling her where we've been keeping him?" Hannah wanted to know.

"Don't worry. I'll manage it."

Hannah, who was sitting at the table, leaned forward and buried her head in her arms. "Oh, brother," she moaned.

"Hannah," Dinnie said firmly, "give Woody a chance."

"Yeah," agreed Faustine. "Besides, Secret is dying."

So Woody went downstairs in search of his mother. It was unusual to find her alone. With ten kids somebody was almost always in her lap or asking her for help or trying to give her help. But Woody found her in the living room paying bills, with only the radio for company.

"Mom?" he said, and then he told her the story of Secret.

Mrs. Rosso was not amused. "And where is this rabbit right now?" she wanted to know.

"He's upstairs," replied Woody.

"You've been keeping him in your room all this time?"

"Well, not exactly. Sort of in . . . Candy's room." That wasn't a lie. Not really.

"Candy and Abbie are in on this?" Mrs. Rosso asked in surprise.

"Well, we all are."

Woody's mother didn't press the issue. She ap-

peared to be thinking. But before she could say anything, Woody spoke up again. "Mom, please can we
keep Secret? But I mean keep him like a regular rabbit? He's getting sick cooped up in the box with no
sunshine or fresh air."

"I should think so," agreed Mrs. Rosso.

"So can we move him downstairs? Take him outside to play?"

Mrs. Rosso shook her head. "No, Woody."

"Mom!" Woody cried. "Why not?"

"You know the rule."

"But I don't understand it."

"Honey, there's nothing to understand. No pets
means *no pets*. You'll have to find another home for
Secret. And fast, please."

Woody stormed upstairs.

"Told you so," said Hannah, who'd been listening.

"You didn't tell me anything," Woody barked at
her. "And the secret room is still a secret. So there."

"But the secret rabbit isn't. And now we can't even
keep him. What are we going to do?"

"Don't worry," snapped Woody. "I'll take care of
it."

The next day Woody returned from school in a
much better mood. He called his brothers and sisters
into the hidden room. "Right after school started this
fall," he said, "this kid in my class, Clarke O'Shea,
well, his dog was hit by a car and killed. He didn't get

another dog, and I can see why, but I thought he might like a different kind of pet. I told him about Secret, and he really wants him. I'm going to give him Secret tomorrow."

"That," said Abbie fondly, "is a very nice idea."

"Yeah," agreed Ira. "It was no fun having a hidden pet, anyway."

So the Halloween party was a success, the Rosso kids gained a secret room (although Candy lost her privacy), and Secret found a home. But Woody and his brothers and sisters were still without a pet.

# CHAPTER FIVE
# *GARDENIA*

For Gardenia and Faustine, the very best thing about moving to the farm was the outdoors. There was really nothing like it. Dinnie couldn't get over the way an early November morning in the country felt. Sometimes she stepped onto the back porch in her robe and slippers so that she could sniff the air while the sky was still gray. On school mornings she and her brothers and sisters usually woke up just as the sun was rising. From the back stoop Dinnie watched the clouds on the horizon change from gray to silvery pink and saw the golden rays of sunshine slice through them, turning the frost on the grass beyond to platinum before melting it away.

The air was biting cold. Dinnie could see her breath and feel her nose and fingertips tingling.

Sometimes she could smell a fire burning in a faraway chimney. But she was always most awed by the silence. In New York it was possible to appreciate a cold early morning seen through a frosty window, but no matter how tightly the window was closed, city sounds floated through. Cars honked, truck gears ground, garbage trucks ate noisy meals, a kid walked by carrying a blasting radio on his shoulder, and it seemed that somebody's car was always in the way of somebody else's. Dinnie couldn't remember a morning when she hadn't heard an enraged shout of "Move ya car!" or "Get outta my place!" The shouts were usually followed by murderous threats.

Much as Dinnie appreciated the sights and silence of the country, she was most excited about the wildlife. In August she and Faustine had spent hours exploring the farm. They had turned over rocks to find worms and grubs and hundred-leggers. They'd climbed trees to find caterpillars and lazy late-summer butterflies. At dusk they'd caught the last of the lightning bugs, but they'd always let them go before the evening was over. As fall caught up with summer and overtook it, they'd watched flocks of birds gather and head south in great gray bunches. Dinnie especially liked the Canada geese. They flew through the sky in even V formation, and the sight was rarely missed because they announced their arrival with noisy honking that was plainly heard in the chilly nighttime silence.

"I do wish we had some bigger animals, though," Dinnie told her twin one day.

"I know," agreed Faustine. "Bugs and wild birds are nice, but a dog would be better."

"Even a fur-fluff would be better." (Fur-fluff was the twins' private word for any small, furry pet, such as a hamster or gerbil.)

"I guess there's no reason to try asking Mom and Dad for a pet again."

Dinnie received an emphatic "rimbald *not*" from her blue-eyed, freckle-faced sister, and that was the end of that discussion.

On the morning after the Halloween party, while Secret was still hidden in the little room upstairs, Mrs. Rosso announced, "We are going to have an old-fashioned Thanksgiving this year. A country Thanksgiving."

The Rossos were gathered in the kitchen in various stages of breakfast.

"What do you mean, Mom?" asked Candy, an eager look in her eyes.

"I mean we're going to celebrate the holiday as it was meant to be celebrated. You might be surprised to know that Thanksgiving isn't just rushing to the Stop and Shop on the day before Thanksgiving and filling your cart with stuffing mix, mashed potato flakes, cans of cranberry jelly and peas, a self-basting Mr. Tom turkey, and a carton of ice cream. There's more to it than that."

Over the next few weeks Dinnie found out just what "more to it" meant. With their mother's help (and with their father's help on the weekends), Dinnie and her brothers and sisters baked pies and made jelly. They made their own apple butter and cranberry relish. While it was fun for everyone, Woody couldn't help saying, "I'm surprised Mom doesn't want a cow so we could milk it and make our own butter."

One day the Rosso kids arrived home from school to find the kitchen table covered from end to end with squashes, gourds, and dried ears of corn. "Time to make the table and door decorations," their mother told them.

But the most interesting thing (for ten city kids) happened the day Mrs. Rosso made her announcement about an old-fashioned Thanksgiving. As soon as breakfast was over and everyone was dressed, the Rossos piled into their van, and Mr. Rosso started down the driveway, a mischievous look in his eyes. "Where are we going? Where are we going?" Jan kept pestering her parents. But they wouldn't answer.

Dinnie glanced at her twin. "Tosh," she whispered. "Groode!" which meant, "A surprise—very exciting!"

Mr. Rosso turned right on the country highway at the end of their drive, stayed on the road for a mile, then turned left into the drive of a neighboring farm. It was the Pritchards' place. Dinnie had met Mr. and Mrs. Pritchard once with her mother. Mr. Pritchard and two farmhands ran a big turkey farm all by themselves. He and his wife looked as old as the hills to Dinnie, but they seemed to work and bake and garden like anyone else.

"The Pritchards' Turkey Farm?" asked Dinnie as the van bumped its way slowly along the rutted gravel drive.

"That's right!" said Mr. Rosso.

The Rosso kids were bursting with questions, but they held them in. A surprise was a surprise.

Wrinkled Mr. Pritchard met the van with a shovel in his hand and a pipe in his mouth. "Right on time," he said gruffly. "I like that."

With a wave of his hand he indicated that the Rossos should follow him, so they did, Ira picking his way carefully through the muddy farmyard. As they rounded a back corner of the barn, they were greeted by an unceasing chorus of gobbling.

"Groode!" said Dinnie under her breath.

Before her was a huge pen crowded with turkeys.

"*Those* are *turkeys?*" exclaimed Jan. "They don't look like turkeys at all!"

"Well, they are," said Mr. Rosso, "and one of them will be ours."

Dinnie's first thought was, "Why are Mom and Dad letting us get a pet?" Then she realized what her father meant. "For Thanksgiving?" she asked.

"That's right," replied her mother. "This is a real treat. We can pick out any turkey we want, and Mr. Pritchard will tag it for us and then fatten it up for Thanksgiving. Our turkey this year will be fresh, not store-bought and frozen. It's up to you kids to decide on one."

Dinnie and her brothers and sisters rushed to the fence around the turkeys. Jan, Ira, and Hannah stood on the lowest rung, peering down. The others rested their arms on the top rung and gazed intently at the flock.

"There's a fat one!" called Bainbridge.

"Where?" asked Ira.

"There."

"Look at that one!" exclaimed Woody. "Ooh, he's tough!"

"There are twelve of us," Abbie pointed out. "We better choose the biggest one we see."

It took a long time to agree on the biggest one, but at last Dinnie pointed out a fat tom strutting through the flock as if he were turkey king. The Rossos agreed that no turkey was bigger than he.

"We'll take him," Mr. Rosso told Mr. Pritchard.

"And we'll name him Goliath," Dinnie added.

"That's not a good idea," muttered Mr. Pritchard, but nobody heard him.

On Monday afternoon Dinnie persuaded the elementary school bus driver to make a stop a mile before the Rossos' farm.

"What are we going to the Pritchards' for?" Faustine asked her twin as they trudged up the pitted driveway.

"To see Goliath, of course," replied Dinnie.

Goliath was as big and imperious as ever.

"I think he's kind of handsome, don't you?" said Dinnie as they leaned over the fence that surrounded the turkeys.

"Kind of," replied Faustine.

On Tuesday they were back again. "Look at him. He's so proud," said Dinnie fondly.

"He has nice manners," added Faustine. "It's crowded in that pen, but Goliath never steps on the other turkeys' feet."

The twins visited Goliath whenever they could. It was the following week, not long after Woody had found a new home for Secret, that Dinnie, resting her chin on the top rung of the turkey pen, said, "It's sad to think that we're going to *eat* old Goliath for Thanksgiving dinner, isn't it?"

"Rimbald brando," replied Faustine. (*Extremely* sad.)

"Maybe we should ask the others if we could choose a different turkey."

"Maybe . . ." said Faustine.

"But—but I don't really want to kill *any* of the turkeys. They're all Goliath's friends."

"But we especially can't kill Goliath," said Faustine.

"No, I don't think we can." Dinnie looked into her sister's face, which was like looking into a mirror. "We better talk to Abbie," she said, and Faustine agreed.

That night Abbie listened patiently to the twins' pleas. "I know how you feel," she said, "but everyone chose Goliath. It's not easy for twelve people to agree on one thing. Besides, I don't think Mom and Dad would be very happy if they had to go back to Mr. Pritchard and explain that we changed our minds—or *why* we changed our minds."

"We won't eat Goliath," said Faustine stubbornly.

Abbie sighed. "Then don't eat him. You can eat stuffing and vegetables and cranberry sauce instead."

"No, you don't understand!" cried Dinnie. "We won't let Goliath be killed. It's cruel! Come on, Faustine."

The twins closed themselves in their bedroom.

"We've got work to do," Dinnie told her sister. "Plans to make."

The other Rossos had no idea what the twins were up to until Saturday. That morning the warm kitchen, which smelled of cloves and pumpkin and baking pie crust, was invaded by a two-person picket line. Dinnie marched around the table carrying a sign that read Save Goliath. She was followed by Faustine with a sign that showed a fat red *X* covering a picture of a cooked turkey.

"What's all this?" asked Mr. Rosso, glancing at his wife.

"We love Goliath," said Dinnie.

"And we don't want him killed for Thanksgiving," Faustine finished up.

"But girls," said Mrs. Rosso, "we can't go back to Mr. Pritchard and tell him you fell in love with the turkey."

The twins shrugged.

"I don't see why not," said Dinnie. Then she led the protest into the living room.

Ira was the first one to crack. "I never thought about the killing part," he confessed with a shudder.

"It *is* kind of mean," added Jan, looking up from a coloring book.

That night Abbie knocked on the twins' bedroom door. "I've been thinking . . ." she began.

The following Monday afternoon three school

buses each stopped a mile down the road from the Rossos' farm. By the time the last one was disappearing in the distance, all ten Rosso kids were gathered around the Pritchards' turkey pen, gazing at Goliath.

"So we'll just choose another turkey," said Hardy practically. "Maybe Mr. Pritchard will let us trade. Look over there. That turkey in the corner is almost as fat as Goliath."

"But we'll still have to kill it," said Ira in a trembling voice.

"*We* don't have to, stupid," said Woody. "Old Mr. Pritchard does that."

"I don't want any of the turkeys to be killed," Jan broke in. "It's mean."

"We don't want them to be killed either," said Dinnie, speaking for Faustine as well.

"Neither do I," said Abbie and Candy at the same time.

"I guess I don't either," said Bainbridge.

"Thanksgiving wouldn't be Thanksgiving without a turkey," said Hardy slowly, "but why do we have to know the turkey we eat ahead of time?"

"Right," said Bainbridge. "I think that's the problem."

The twins glanced at each other, satisfied.

"I could eat a turkey from the freezer of Stop and Shop, I think," said Dinnie. "I'd know it was a turkey and someone had to kill it, but we wouldn't have known the bird ahead of time. Besides, turkeys in freezers don't even look like turkeys. They look like frosted plastic bags."

"Is it agreed then?" said Abbie. "We'll tell Mr. Pritchard we've changed our minds and won't be needing Goliath after all."

"Agreed!" said Dinnie joyously.

The Rossos found Mr. Pritchard and one of his farmhands repairing the fencing around a pigsty.

"Well, well," said Mr. Pritchard, glancing up and seeing the ten kids coming toward him. He squinted fiercely into the sun. "Checking on that bird of yours again?"

Abbie stepped forward. "Yes sir," she replied. "And we have to tell you something."

"What's that?" Mr. Pritchard was still squatting on the ground. He slid his hat back, scratched his head, and stood up.

"Well . . . sir . . . we, um, we won't be needing him after all."

"You won't, eh? Why is that?"

"Well . . . our plans have changed. We hope you won't mind too much."

Mr. Pritchard frowned and rubbed the white stubble on his chin. "I guess not," he said. "I'm sure someone else will want the bird. I don't think I'll have any trouble selling him again."

Horror washed over Dinnie. They weren't saving

Goliath after all. She squeezed between Hannah and Faustine and pushed her way forward until she was next to Abbie. "Wait a sec," she exclaimed. "We— we'll take him after all. But we'll take him alive."

"It was the only thing I could think of," Dinnie told her brothers and sisters desperately as they were walking home later. "I know we can't save all the turkeys, but as least we can save Goliath."

"But Dinnie, Mom is going to be doubly mad," Abbie pointed out. "She'll have to buy a store turkey, *and* she'll be stuck with a live turkey when she's told us hundreds of times 'no pets.'"

"We'll just have to convince her to let us keep him," Dinnie persisted. "We'll wait until he arrives. She won't be able to say no. It'll almost be Thanksgiving then. She'll have to show some holiday spirit."

Somehow everybody "forgot" to tell Mr. and Mrs. Rosso that they would need to add a frozen turkey to their shopping list. Then, early in the morning on the day before Thanksgiving, the Pritchard Turkey Farm truck drove up the Rossos' driveway, and one of the farmhands jumped out of the cab. He hurried around to the back of the truck, lifted a crate off, and deposited it by the Rossos' stoop.

Mrs. Rosso stuck her head out the door in surprise. "But that's a *live* turkey!" she exclaimed.

"The children said you'd changed your mind, ma'am," replied the farmhand. He touched his hat, then climbed into the cab, backed the truck around noisily, and headed down the drive.

Mrs. Rosso turned to find Dinnie and Faustine watching her sheepishly.

"Do you know anything about this?" she asked, closing the door behind her with a blast of chilly air. She sounded more confused than angry.

Dinnie grasped Faustine's hand. "Borderish," she muttered helplessly.

"Don't you think we should let that turkey out?" asked Faustine carefully, taking a step toward the door. "We can't just—"

"Not until I find out what that man meant when he said, 'The *children* said you'd changed your mind,'" replied Mrs. Rosso. "Into the kitchen."

While Faustine helped her mother with the table-setting system, Dinnie slumped in a chair and told Mrs. Rosso the entire story of Goliath.

Mr. Rosso came into the kitchen in time to hear the end of the story, threw on his hat, coat, scarf, and gloves, and flew out the door in search of a frozen turkey.

Mrs. Rosso tried to remain calm and patient, but she was having difficulty. "I know how you feel about animals, Gardenia," she said, "but you should have told me what was going on. You are not the only one eating Thanksgiving dinner. Getting a fresh turkey was my idea. I should have had some say in the matter."

Dinnie hung her head. "I know," she replied.

"It wasn't just your fault, though," Mrs. Rosso went on. "All of you kept quiet. Abbie and Bainbridge should have known better."

"We all *wanted* to tell you, Mom," said Dinnie. "I guess we were just afraid for Goliath."

Mrs. Rosso patted Dinnie's knee. "Well, your hearts were in the right place," she said. "Now let's just hope your father finds something big enough for the twelve of us."

While they waited for Mr. Rosso to return, Mrs. Rosso gathered all the children and told them exactly what she thought about what they had done. She gave Abbie and Bainbridge an extra talking-to because they were the oldest. It wasn't really fair, but that's what happened. The oldest were supposed to know better.

Mr. Rosso came home empty-handed. "Sorry," he told his family. "I drove to five supermarkets. There's not a turkey to be had. Everyone's already bought theirs."

"Not a single turkey?" repeated Woody pitifully.

"Well, actually I did find *one*, but it was about the size of a baseball. While I was trying to decide whether there was any point in taking it, somebody else bought it."

"Then I guess we'll have a vegetarian dinner this year." Mrs. Rosso looked around the kitchen at the vegetables and cornbread and muffins and pies. "There's certainly plenty to eat without Goliath."

"Goliath!" exclaimed Dinnie, remembering. "He's still out there in that crate."

"Hey," said Woody, "maybe Mr. Pritchard could come over and . . . you know. I bet there's time."

"*No.*" Nine pairs of angry eyes bored into him.

"Okay, okay, okay," said Woody.

"Bainbridge, why don't you and Dinnie go outside and fix Goliath up somewhere," suggested Mr. Rosso.

"Does that mean we can keep him?!" cried Dinnie.

"Absolutely not," replied her mother. "But there's nothing we can do about him until after tomorrow, so we might as well make him comfortable somewhere. I suppose you know everything about keeping a turkey? What he eats, how much space he needs?"

"Not exactly," replied Dinnie.

"Then call Mr. Pritchard and find out, honey. He's your responsibility."

So once again the Rossos had a temporary pet. But first thing Friday morning Mrs. Rosso announced, "Time to find a proper home for Goliath. Since all you kids saved his neck, you may all participate in the search. But Dinnie, I'm appointing you head of the Find a Home for Goliath Committee."

Most of the rest of Dinnie's Thanksgiving vacation

was spent poring through the ads in the local papers with her brothers and sisters and making phone calls. Every call led to a dead end, until Abbie, momentarily distracted by a page of department store ads, saw the announcement that read: "Hillsborough Mall—100 Stores! Restaurants! Movies! Exhibits! And Now—Bring the Kids to Our New *Petting Zoo!*"

"See? A petting zoo," said Abbie after she'd read the ad to the others. "Maybe they'd like a nice tom turkey."

"A nice, *polite* tom turkey," added Faustine.

"Well, we'll find out," replied Dinnie.

After several phone calls she reached the woman in charge of the petting zoo, who was delighted with the donation of Goliath and even sent someone out to the Rossos' farm to pick him up.

"Come visit him anytime you want," called the man before he drove off.

"We will!" Dinnie called back.

And she did—many times. But a pet at the petting zoo was not at all the same as a pet of her own at home.

# CHAPTER SIX
# *JANTHINA*

"I love Christmas, I love snow." Janthina Rosso hummed busily. She tried hard to remember the song Mr. Heppler, her first-grade teacher, had sung the other day.

Jan was filling in a worksheet for school. It was all about Christmas, but that didn't fool her. A worksheet was work whether it showed the alphabet or pictures of Santa Claus. And this worksheet was *home*work. No fair. Jan was sure Ira had never had homework when *he* was in first grade.

Jan paused and sucked on the end of her green crayon. She hoped the crayon would make a spot on her front tooth. Then she could walk around smiling, and all day people would say, "Jan, you've got a piece of spinach on your tooth," and Jan could laugh and show them it was just crayon.

Jan looked at her worksheet again. She had finished two rows. The third row showed a picture of a bell with an *X* over it. Next to the bell were a candle, a wreath, and a bow. Jan knew she was supposed to make an *X* over the bow, since it was the other *B* word, and color in the candle and the wreath. She looked down the page. Four more rows. This worksheet would take forever! Maybe one of her brothers or sisters would finish it for her. They usually did anything she asked.

Jan wandered into the kitchen, which was warm and smelled of gingerbread. Hannah was the only one there, busy doing her homework. You never knew what to expect when you asked Hannah a question, but Jan decided to try anyway. "Hannah, will you finish my worksheet for me?"

"A-*hem!*"

Jan spun around. Her mother was standing in the doorway. "Janthina, it is Friday afternoon, and you have plenty of time to do your homework. Besides, your homework is for *you* to do, not anyone else. Why don't you finish it right now? We have lots of Christmas things to do this weekend."

"We do?"

"Yes. We're going to get our tree, remember?"

"Oh, yes!"

Christmas, Christmas, Christmas! It was Jan's favorite time of the year. And here in the country, Christmas somehow seemed more special than in New York City. Jan had to admit that it wasn't quite as exciting—no glittering store windows everywhere you turned, no Santa Clauses on every corner—but it was more fun.

One day, shortly after the man from the petting zoo had come for Goliath, Mrs. Rosso had given a "country Christmas" speech that wasn't too different from her "country Thanksgiving" speech, and Jan had paid close attention.

"We are going to become do-it-yourselfers," Mrs. Rosso had said. "We are going to make our own decorations and some of our own presents. We're going to chop down our own Christmas tree, and make wreaths from holly and laurel and evergreens, and do our baking from scratch."

"Can we still use the electricity?" asked Woody.

Mrs. Rosso laughed. "Of course we can. And we'll put up the store-bought decorations we already have. And we'll have to buy most of the materials and ingredients we need. I just want you kids to see that Christmas isn't all department stores and electronic toys and things that come out of boxes and grocery bags."

"Anyone who wants to use my tools is welcome," added Mr. Rosso. "I'll be glad to give you a hand if you want to make gifts or decorations in the workshop. There's just one thing. I'm going to be working on a secret project—let's call it Project X—in the basement. I'll keep it away from the workshop when I'm not busy with it. I'll cover it with a sheet. And I expect you not to peek. Is that clear?"

Mr. Rosso tried to sound stern, but Jan could see that his eyes were dancing and his mouth was twitching. "It's clear," said Jan, and everyone laughed, since Jan had such a terrible time keeping secrets, hers or anyone else's. "Who's Project X for?" she wanted to know.

"My lips are sealed," said Mr. Rosso. "So no peeking. And if you see a sign on the basement door that says Project X, don't come downstairs. That means I'm working on it."

"It's probably another wall unit," Jan heard Woody whisper to Hardy.

From that day on there were mini-workshops throughout the farmhouse. The kitchen table was almost always covered with cookie decorations and cookie cutters and spices and flour. A table was set up in the den for card making. A table in the family room became the ornament-making center. And a table in the messy mudroom was where Mrs. Rosso worked on her evergreen wreaths.

Jan sighed and sat down next to Hannah to finish her worksheet.

The next afternoon, after a lunch of hot soup, the twelve Rossos put on their outdoor clothes. "It's only twenty-eight degrees today," said Ira, glancing at the thermometer.

"Hats for everyone, then," Mrs. Rosso announced.

When the kids were bundled up to her satisfaction, the Rossos set out across the farmyard. Mr. Rosso stopped in the shed for an ax, a saw, and Jan and Ira's sled, and then they trudged through the woods.

A dusting of snow, not even enough to cover the oak leaves on the ground, had fallen the night before. It didn't crunch underfoot or smush into snowballs, but it was a nice snow, Jan thought. It made the woods look Christmasy.

"'Whose woods these are'," said Candy, quoting a Robert Frost poem as they walked along, "'I think I know. His house is in the village, though.'"

"Let's sing Christmas songs!" suggested Jan, watching her foggy breath puff away in front of her.

"Great," said Hannah. "Here's a good one. 'We three kings of Orient are, smoking on a rubber cigar. It was loaded and explo-oded—'"

"*Hannah*," said Mr. Rosso warningly, as Woody and Hardy dissolved into laughter.

"Daddy, I don't know that one," Jan complained,

and couldn't understand why her sisters and brothers (except Ira) laughed at that, too.

"Never mind, Jan," Ira whispered.

"Bainbridge, will you pull me on the sled?" Jan asked pitifully.

"Sure," he replied, helping her on.

"You kids are supposed to be looking for a tree," Mrs. Rosso reminded them.

"Looking for a tree!" exclaimed Hannah. "We're surrounded!"

"You know what I mean."

"There are lots of fir trees farther ahead," said Faustine. The twins had spent more time in the woods than anyone else had.

Sure enough, the Rossos soon came to a small grove of evergreens.

"Wow!" cried Abbie. "Look at this tree! It's perfect."

"No, look at *this* one," said Hardy.

"Here's a big one," said Bainbridge.

"Not *too* tall," Mr. Rosso cautioned. "It has to fit in the living room."

It was Jan who finally found a tree that everyone agreed on. It was neither too tall nor too squat, too skinny nor too wide, and the needles were the perfect length for showing off ornaments.

Bainbridge whacked at the trunk with an ax.

"Oh! I hear it crying!" exclaimed Dinnie.

"You do not," said Jan, but she felt a little sorry for the tree, too. What could she do, though? You had to have a tree for Santa to leave presents under.

When Bainbridge had made a notch in the tree, the others took turns sawing through the trunk. The tree began to wobble and lean and at last . . .

"Timber!" cried Hannah, but her father caught the tree before it hit the ground.

Mr. Rosso laid it on the sled. "Only the tree gets a ride back," he told Jan. "You can walk alongside and hold it in place if you want."

"Since it's my tree, I better."

"It is not your tree, you just—" Hannah began.

But Mrs. Rosso put a stop to the argument. "We'll make hot chocolate when we get home," she announced.

Everyone picked up the pace. When they reached the farmhouse, Mrs. Rosso and Jan, Ira, Hannah, and the twins started the hot chocolate while the other kids helped Mr. Rosso stand the tree in a bucket of water on the back stoop and spray its branches with Wilt-Pruf.

"Why is my tree outside, Mommy?" asked Jan.

"We have to leave it there until it's a little closer to Christmas. If we bring it inside now, it'll dry out, and its needles will fall off."

"Ew," replied Jan. But she gazed proudly at her tree. And every morning and every night until the

Rossos brought it inside, she stepped onto the stoop to see that it was all right.

Jan was counting the days to Christmas, and there weren't too many left. Just eleven. Not bad, considering she'd started with fifty-eight. Jan wasn't sure what *that* meant, but she did know that the farmhouse was full of secrets. Her father was working away at Project X in the basement. Jan often heard hammering and tapping and sawing and the rasping sound of the plane as it smoothed rough edges. Everywhere she went, someone cried, "Don't look!" or "Close your eyes!" or "Don't come in!" There were closets labeled Do Not Enter and No Peeking!

Jan had secrets of her own. Some were homemade, as her mother wanted, and some were store-bought. She was very proud that she had presents, or ideas for presents, for every member of her family. Eleven presents were a lot. And she had made very special Christmas cards for her grandparents and Mr. Heppler.

Jan's best homemade present was for her mother. She had found some stencils and painted fruit designs onto jar lids to make beautiful coasters for when company came. Her best store-bought present was for Abbie. Abbie liked jewelry, so Jan had bought her a pair of earrings with long blue feathers on them. They were gorgeous. And they had cost almost two dollars. Jan had wrapped them and put them under her bed with her other presents.

Jan noticed that year that the closer Christmas came, the harder it was to sleep. She never knew when Santa Claus might be out making a trial run. It would be so exciting to see him! One night Jan awoke with a start. She thought she had heard something. Sleigh bells jingling? Rudolph pawing at the eaves? Jan leaped out of bed. She ran to the window. She saw only the moon shining on another feeble dusting of snow, and heard only... *rap, rap, rap*. It was her father in his workshop.

Jan knew she wouldn't be able to fall asleep until the house was silent. She tiptoed into the hall. Since she couldn't tell time, she had no idea how late it was. The doors to the bedrooms of her brothers and sisters were closed, although a light was on in the big girls' room. But the door to her parents' room was open, and their bed was still made.

Jan crept downstairs. The hammering grew louder. She reached the door to the basement and saw the Project X sign. Well, that was that. She couldn't go any farther. She knew better than to intrude on Project X. As Jan stood there, the hammering stopped, and she heard voices. Her mother was in the basement, too.

Jan couldn't help listening for a few moments.

She'd been so good about not going in closets or lifting the Project X sheet.

" . . . kids . . . ," she heard her mother say. And then something about Christmas.

Her father's voice was louder. ". . . never guess it's a doghouse."

Jan's heart began to pound as loudly as her father's hammer. A doghouse! If her father was building a doghouse, it could mean only one thing. Mrs. Rosso had changed her mind about a pet, and Jan and her brothers and sisters were being given a dog—probably a puppy—for Christmas. That truly was a surprise! It would be the best surprise of their lives. No wonder Jan's father had made such a big deal about Project X.

Jan ran back up the stairs and down the hall and jumped into her bed. She wished Ira or Hannah were awake because she was bursting with her news. Then she remembered that Project X was a secret, and that she shouldn't tell what she had found out. With great difficulty Jan managed to fall asleep again, and she dreamed about puppies all night.

The next morning Jan kept the amazing secret while she got ready for school. She kept it during breakfast. She kept it while Mrs. Rosso shooed the ten children out the door in alphabetical order. But the secret didn't last much longer. By the time Jan reached the bus stop, she truly thought she was going to explode. She wriggled around like a puppy, and hopped from one foot to the other.

"Guys?" Jan said, addressing all of her brothers and sisters.

No one was paying attention.

"Guys? . . . *Guys? . . . I found out what Project X is!*"

Woody and Hardy stopped punching each other. Hannah stopped teasing the twins.

"I have to tell you!" exclaimed Jan. "I just have to. It is *so good!* I accidentally heard Mommy and Daddy talking last night, and Project X is . . . a doghouse!"

"A doghouse? Are you sure?" cried Hannah.

"It *is* shaped like a doghouse," said Hardy slowly, thinking of the sheet-covered form he'd seen in the basement.

"I'm very sure," said Jan. "So that means we're probably getting a puppy for Christmas."

The Rosso kids looked at each other excitedly.

"I wonder what made Mom change her mind," mused Abbie.

"Who cares? Don't knock it," said Woody. "Maybe Dad made her change her mind. *He's* never said ten kids is enough."

"We can't let Mom and Dad know that we know about Project X, though," Bainbridge reminded the others. "Okay? That's *our* secret."

"Okay," agreed his brothers and sisters.

"Oh, let's buy the puppy some presents!" said

Candy. "We could get it a leash and a collar and a food dish. Then we'll be ready for it. Our puppy should have some presents on Christmas, too."

The Rosso kids were very busy the next few days. When Mrs. Rosso drove into town, Bainbridge and Candy went with her. They had collected money from all of the kids, and they secretly bought some puppy supplies. Abbie began knitting a blanket for the puppy. Jan and Ira wrapped the puppy's presents. The presents would have to stay hidden, though, until after the puppy had made his appearance.

"We better choose a name for our puppy," Jan told Ira and Hannah as they were getting ready for bed one chilly night.

"Right," said Hannah. "Let's talk to the others."

The kids met in the twins' room.

"We need a boy's name and a girl's name," said Jan.

"But we are *not* going to look in *What Shall We Name the Baby?*" said Abbie. "I'll never forget when Mom found out she was going to have twins, and she opened that awful book and saw that the girls' names would be Faustine and Gardenia."

"What were the boys' names?" asked Dinnie curiously.

"Farley and Galen." Abbie made a gagging sound.

"You mean I could have been named *Farley?*" shrieked Faustine.

"It's not as bad as Dagwood," said Woody.

"Well, anyway," said Abbie, "we'll decide on nice, normal names for the puppy. And we won't even *think* about *Name the Baby.*"

"I like Sally," said Jan.

"Mary," said Abbie.

"Tom," said Ira.

"John," said Woody.

"A puppy named John?" asked Bainbridge.

The Rossos decided to name the puppy after they had seen it.

Christmas Eve that year was a crystal-clear, starry night.

"No snow for Christmas," said Ira, sounding disappointed.

"But this is better," said Jan. "Santa won't get lost. He and Rudolph will be able to see where they're going." And I'll be able to see them, she thought.

Abbie and Bainbridge hid smiles. It had been a long time since they'd believed in Santa.

Jan was sure she wouldn't be able to sleep at all on Christmas Eve. The day had already been exciting, and so many more exciting things would happen while she was in bed. The tree had been trimmed several days earlier, but on Christmas Eve Mr. Rosso had turned on its lights for the first time. Jan had looked at her little tree standing in the corner of the living room in a haze of soft, glowing color and thought she'd never seen anything so beautiful.

Then Jan and the rest of the kids had brought all of their presents out of secret hiding places and arranged them under the tree. They'd sung Christmas carols and had eggnog (Jan had spit hers out), and then Jan had set out a plate of cookies for Santa Claus.

Finally, Mrs. Rosso had said, "Time for bed, kids!" and Jan hadn't objected. Santa would come only after she'd gone to sleep. Then he'd slide down the chimney and fill the twelve stockings and pile more presents under the tree. Before he left he'd stop to eat Jan's snack. Oh, it was so exciting! How could Jan possibly fall asleep?

But she did. And when she awoke in the gray dawn of Christmas, she realized she'd slept very soundly. She didn't remember hearing sleigh bells or hooves pawing the roof or a jolly voice calling out, "Happy Christmas to all and to all a good night!"

But who cared? It was Christmas!

"Merry Christmas!" cried Jan. "Merry Christmas!"

Hannah and Ira were up in a flash. "Come on!" said Hannah.

The three youngest Rosso children ran through the second floor hallway, knocking on bedroom doors. "It's Christmas!" they shouted.

Everyone woke up quickly, even Abbie, who had said she was too old to get excited about Christmas anymore. But Mr. Rosso wouldn't allow anyone downstairs until he'd lit their Christmas morning fire and made a pot of coffee.

After what seemed like days to Jan, her father called, "Okay, everybody!"

The kids were lined up on the steps in reverse alphabetical order—Jan first, Abbie last. They ran downstairs. Jan was greeted by stuffed stockings and mounds of gifts. She was glad there were twelve people in her family because she liked the sight of lots and lots of presents.

For the next couple of hours Jan and her brothers and sisters untied ribbons and ripped through wrapping paper. Jan got her very own microphone so she could pretend she was singing on a stage, a sweater knitted by Mrs. Rosso, a doctor's kit and uniform, and a jigsaw specially made by Hardy. The living room of the Rosso's house was filled with oohs and aahs. But when the last gift had been opened, no doghouse (or puppy) was in sight.

"What do you know?" Mr. Rosso said suddenly to Mrs. Rosso. "I believe there's one more gift. We forgot something."

Jan watched her father disappear into the basement. A few minutes later he returned with Project X in his arms. It was still covered with the sheet. He set it in front of Jan. "This is for you, sweetie," he said. "Merry Christmas!"

"For *me?*" Jan couldn't believe it. The puppy was

going to be hers! She wondered where it was hidden.

Jan pulled the sheet up carefully.

Underneath was a spectacular . . . dollhouse.

"A *doll*house?" exclaimed Jan. What had happened? She had misunderstood something.

A moment of stunned silence followed. Abbie broke it. "Oh, Dad, it's beautiful!" she cried. "Isn't it, Jan?"

"Yes . . . beautiful," Jan managed to say. And it was. It was the dollhouse of Jan's dreams. It's just that it wasn't a doghouse. But Jan tried to look thrilled anyway.

Christmas Day was so full of new toys and phone calls and visitors that Jan and her brothers and sisters were able to cover up their disappointment easily. That night they put the puppy's Christmas presents in the attic. Christmas was over, and Jan had a dollhouse, but the Rossos were still without a pet.

# CHAPTER SEVEN
# *EBERHARD*

Eberhard Rosso's heart was racing. A blizzard! Had he heard right? The weather forecaster had just predicted a *blizzard*.

It was a Tuesday in January, three weeks after Christmas, and Hardy and his brothers had come home from school.

"We've hardly had any snow since we moved here," Hardy remarked. "Just little dustings. Look outside. Not a flake in sight."

Woody shrugged. He reached across Hardy to change the station on the radio.

"Hey! Leave it alone!" cried Hardy. "I want to hear the next weather report."

"You can hear it later. If there's going to be a blizzard, we'll know about it. But this station is really boring."

"Don't touch it!"

"Don't touch *me!*"

"Hey, you guys," said Bainbridge. "Be quiet. I have to start my homework."

Woody shot both of his brothers a murderous look, then raised his hand to karate-chop the radio. Bainbridge caught his hand on its way down.

"If you break that, little brother, I'll break—"

"*Shh!*" hissed Hardy. "Listen!"

". . . winter storm warnings are in effect," the newscaster on the radio was saying. "We might see as much as two feet of snow. And high winds will cause drifting of up to five feet. We're really going to get it this time, folks!" he added. "Please stay tuned for further details."

Hardy stared at his brothers in awe. "Whoa," was all he could say.

But the next morning didn't seem very promising, blizzard-wise.

"Will you look at that," said Hardy in disgust, peering out of the boys' bedroom window at the thermometer on the side of the house. "Forty-three degrees. How's it supposed to snow at that temperature? And look at the sky. It's gray, all right, but I've seen worse. I know what's going to happen. They're going to get us all psyched up for a blizzard, and then we'll have about two inches of snow—maybe less—and they won't even have to close school."

"Would you chill out?" said Bainbridge. "Finish getting dressed. We're going to be late for breakfast."

"I want to hear the weather again first," Hardy replied, reaching for the radio. But before he could turn it on, a shriek came from Abbie and Candy's room.

"What is it? What's wrong?" Woody, Hardy, and Bainbridge dashed into their sisters' room.

"A blizzard! We're going to get a blizzard!" cried Candy. "Isn't that romantic?"

"You mean they're still predicting the blizzard?" asked Hardy. Excitement shot through him. "What did they say?"

"They said the temperature's supposed to drop all day, accompanied by thickening clouds and rising winds," Candy replied.

"What'd you do?" Woody interrupted. "Memorize the report?"

"Ignore him, Candy," said Abbie. "Go on."

"Snow is supposed to start falling by midnight tonight and go on for who knows how long."

"All right!" whooped Hardy. "All *right!*"

Sure enough, the temperature did drop that day. It was well into the twenties by the time Hardy and the other elementary school kids got off their bus and started up the drive to the Rossos' farmhouse.

"It's going to snow for sure," said Faustine, sniffing the air. "I can smell it."

"And I can feel it," added Dinnie, rubbing her wrist. Dinnie had once broken her wrist badly, and now it let her know with a dull ache whenever rain or snow was on the way.

"Wind's picking up, too," said Hardy, looking at the lashing treetops.

"Poor birds," said Faustine. "I always feel sorry for the birds and wild animals when it snows. They have such a hard time finding food."

"Yeah," agreed Hannah.

"And they have to *sleep* in the snow," Jan pointed out. "Yuck."

A gust of wind blew a dirty paper cup against Ira's foot. "Litterbugs," he muttered. He picked up the cup gingerly and held it away from him as he and the others hurried toward the house, heads bent into the wind.

Mrs. Rosso greeted them with hugs and hot chocolate. "Snow's on the way," she said. "We'll have to batten down the hatches tonight."

"What do you mean?" asked Hardy.

"Make sure everything in the yard is put away or tied down. It wouldn't hurt to close the shutters on the house, either. Apparently, we're in for a doozy.

I'm going to drive into town now and buy some candles and canned food, just in case. Anyone want to come with me?"

"I do!" cried the younger children. But Hardy decided to stay at home where he could keep an eye on the storm.

Not much happened that afternoon, though, except that the wind began to howl around the corners of the farmhouse, and night seemed to fall quickly as the sky grew darker and heavier with clouds.

Mrs. Rosso and Jan, Ira, and Hannah returned with bags of supplies, and Mr. Rosso came home from work somewhat earlier than usual. "It's as dark as a pocket out there," he said, "and as cold as a witch's nose."

That night Mrs. Rosso fixed chickens for dinner. (If she planned things just right, the twelve Rossos could eat exactly two whole large chickens at a meal.) Afterward, Hardy trailed through the house, following his father, who was closing the shutters and checking nooks and crannies for cracks that might let the snow in.

"Better start your homework, son," said Mr. Rosso absently.

Hardy was much too excited to settle down with his homework. Besides, he was sure he didn't need to do it. "Aw, Dad, we won't have school tomorrow."

"You never know. Better get to it."

Hardy did a patchwork job on his math, jumping up every few minutes to look out the window. By the time he went to bed at ten o'clock, not a flake of snow had fallen. But the wind was so fierce that it rattled the shutters and whistled down the chimney in the living room.

Like Jan on Christmas Eve, Hardy was sure he wouldn't be able to fall asleep, but he did, almost immediately, and when he awoke, it was the next morning—five minutes before the boys' alarm clock was set to go off. Hardy rolled out of bed, his feet hitting the floor with a thud, and made a grab for the window shade. It snapped up, and Hardy carefully opened the window and the shutters. He was nearly blinded—not by the glare of sunlight but by a world turned white.

"It's the blizzard!" Hardy shouted. "It's here!"

"Mmphh?" mumbled Bainbridge and Woody from their beds.

"It's the blizzard!" Hardy was in awe of what he saw outside the window. The farmyard was blanketed with a thick covering of snow, and more was falling, although to Hardy the snow looked less as if it were falling than as if it were being hurled from the clouds in angry handfuls. He had never seen anything like it. The snow came teeming and whirling down, and while a regular old snowfall is quiet, this storm was noisy. The wind continued to roar and howl as it lashed the snow to the ground.

"Oh, boy," murmured Hardy, closing the window. "No school today. That's for sure." But he knew he had to check, so he turned the radio on softly and tuned it to a local station.

". . . everything closed up tight as a drum here in Mercer County," the announcer was saying. "All schools are closed. I repeat, all public, private, and parochial schools in Mercer County are *closed* today."

Hardy let out a whoop, turned off the alarm clock, and, leaving his sleeping brothers behind, ran downstairs and into the kitchen. He found his parents, Candy, and the younger children already there.

"Snow day! Snow day!" cried Hardy.

The morning was spent doing just what Hardy liked best on an unexpected vacation from school. With the snow whirling and blowing and drifting outside, he and his brothers and sisters crowded onto the couches in the family room with blankets and watched reruns of "I Love Lucy" and "Leave It to Beaver" and "Gilligan's Island." Later in the morning they watched game shows—"Jeopardy" and "Wheel of Fortune" and "Concentration."

Mr. Rosso, who hadn't even been able to get the back door open after breakfast, happily spent the morning in his workshop, while Mrs. Rosso organized two closets and put the contents of a photo album into chronological order.

Late in the afternoon Hardy, Woody, and the twins bundled up in outdoor clothes. After Dinnie squeezed through the tiny opening they were able to create by heaving against the back door, they shoveled off the stoop and decided on a walk to the barn, just to see what it was like during a storm. But the wind blew the snow against their faces in stinging gusts, and they couldn't see for more than a few inches. Disappointed, they returned to the house.

Not much later the announcement came over the radio that school would be closed the next day as well. "A four-day weekend!" Hardy was beside himself with pleasure.

That night the electricity went off. "I'm glad of the candles we bought," said Mrs. Rosso, "but I'm afraid we're going to freeze to death."

Bainbridge and Abbie built a fire in the living room fireplace, and the Rossos gathered around it with blankets. They toasted popcorn in the candlelit room. When the popcorn was gone, a hush fell over them. Hardy listened to the wind whistling and the fire crackling and Ira breathing next to him. Then he heard something else.

"What was that?" asked Faustine.

"I don't know. But I heard it too," Hardy told her.

"You guys are—" Bainbridge started to say, when a crash sounded outside that no one could miss.

"I better go check," said Mr. Rosso, getting to his feet.

"I'll go with you," said Mrs. Rosso.

None of the kids wanted to be left behind. They followed their parents in a nervous bunch.

Mr. Rosso took the biggest flashlight he could find and shined it out the back door.

"Garbage can's knocked over!" exclaimed Hardy.

The garbage cans had been moved against the side of the house the afternoon before. Now one was tipped partway over, the lid off, garbage spilling into the snow.

"Maybe an escaped prisoner is on the loose!" cried Hannah. "Maybe he's trying to get into our house."

"Mommy, really?" whimpered Jan.

"Of course not, honey. Hannah, don't say things like that, please."

The rest of the evening was quiet, and by bedtime the power had been restored, but Hardy couldn't stop thinking about the garbage can. Who or what had turned it over? Hardy had a real mystery to solve— just like Frank and Joe Hardy.

The next morning he got to work right after breakfast. He put on his outdoor clothes, replacing his wool hat with his Sherlock Holmes hat. Then he slipped a magnifying glass into his pocket and squeezed out the back door. His mother handed him a shovel. "See if you can dig us out while you look for clues," she said.

"Aw, Mom, it's still snowing," Hardy replied, but he began work on a path from the back door to the drive.

The snow *was* still falling but not as heavily, and the wind had died down. Hardy figured that at least a foot and a half of snow was on the ground. He saw a few drifts that were as tall as he was.

As he shoveled, he looked for clues, but of course any clues from the night before—footprints or lost buttons or bits of clothing—were long covered by snow. When Hardy finished the path, he examined the trash cans and the side of the house with his magnifying glass, but he didn't see anything except big-looking garbage.

That night the Rossos, who were beginning to have what Mrs. Rosso called "cabin fever," played board games by the fireplace. Jan and Ira were playing checkers, and Jan was just shouting, "King me! King me!" when Hardy heard a noise again.

"Shh," he said, sitting up straight. "I heard something."

The room grew silent.

*Clink. Clank. Clink.*

This time the sounds came from the front of the house.

Everyone ran to the front door, and Mr. Rosso

thrust it open while Mrs. Rosso turned on the porch lights. The yard was empty.

"The chain on the bird feeder is swaying," Hannah pointed out.

"It must be getting windy again," said Hardy.

"I wonder why we didn't hear the chain before," mused Abbie.

No one knew.

When Hardy woke up on Saturday morning, he discovered that the snow had stopped falling. Now I can do some real detective work, he thought. He put on his plaid hat and found his magnifying glass. Then he tiptoed out of the house. He didn't want to get stuck with any more shoveling. He bet Frank and Joe Hardy's father never made *them* shovel snow while they were working on a case.

Hardy looked at the garbage cans again. He dug through the snow around them. He found some crumbs and toast crusts and orange peels, but no buttons or matchbooks or shreds of clothing.

He walked across the yard. Not a human footprint anywhere, just some slender tracks. The tracks circled the house. Hardy followed them. When he reached the back again, he nearly whooped with joy —until he realized the human footprints he had just found were his own.

"Darn," said Hardy.

He investigated the bird feeder. Seed was everywhere.

"Messy birds," he said. "Unless . . ." An idea began
to form in Hardy's mind. He took another look at the
garbage cans. Then he followed his footprints to the
bird feeder, keeping an eye on the smaller tracks beside him.

"Mm-hm, mm-hm," he muttered.

The skinny tracks circled the post that supported
the feeder. Then they angled off across the farmyard
and into the woods.

"Oh, no," Hardy said softly. Then, "*Oh, no!*" He
ran through the deep snow as fast as he was able,
which wasn't very fast, and burst through the back
door of the house and into the kitchen.

"Mom!" he shouted. "Dad! Everybody!"

Most of the Rossos were in the kitchen, pouring
glasses of orange juice and filling cereal bowls.

"Hardy!" said Mrs. Rosso sharply. "What's the
matter? And why are you wearing your boots in the
kitchen? You're dripping everywhere. Go back in the
mudroom and take them off, please."

"But I solved the mystery," Hardy cried, "and
we're all in trouble. Dad, call the police!"

"Boots," said Mrs. Rosso, pointing to Hardy's feet.

"Mom, we're in *trouble!*"

"*Boots.*"

"Why are we in trouble?" asked Faustine nervously.

She glanced at Dinnie and murmured, "Messo-smash."

Dinnie looked back at her twin with frightened eyes.

"Hannah was right," said Hardy, standing his ground. "There *is* an escaped convict. And he's been hanging around our house. Now he's off in the woods somewhere."

"How do you know there's an escaped convict?" asked Mr. Rosso. "Have you been listening to the radio?"

"No," replied Hardy, "but all the clues are right in our yard. The only garbage outside the cans is food. The guy is hungry. He didn't find much in the cans, though, so he walked around the house looking for other stuff. On the way, he crashed into the bird feeder and ate some seed. That's what we heard last night. Then he must have gotten nervous, so he ran into the woods."

"Are you saying there are footprints in our yard?" asked Mrs. Rosso, who now seemed truly concerned, and apparently had forgotten about Hardy's wet boots.

"Well, there are prints," Hardy replied, "but not footprints. They're stilt prints. See, the convict is very clever, and he knows the police could trace him by his footprints, so he's walking on a pair of stilts. They left skinny holes all around the yard."

Bainbridge let out a guffaw, and Woody spit out a mouthful of milk, spraying it across the table at Faustine.

"Ew, ew!" Faustine cried, grabbing for a napkin.

"This convict was walking on *stilts* through the *snow?*" Bainbridge snorted with laughter.

"Boots," Mrs. Rosso ordered Hardy.

"Aren't you going to call the police, Dad?" Hardy wanted to know.

"I don't think so."

"But that guy's probably right out there in the woods."

"Yeah, polishing his stilts," said Woody with a grin.

"Boy," said Hardy. "I do all this work, and everyone laughs at me." He stomped into the mudroom.

Hardy stayed mad at the Rossos all day. Just to prove how stupid they were, he wore his plaid hat all day, too. It would remind them that he was a detective.

It was late in the afternoon, as dusk was falling, that Hardy found the real solution to the mystery. *Clink, clank, clink* went the chain on the feeder again. Hardy rushed to the window by the front door. Then he rushed around the house, rounding up his family. "Hey, you guys! Hey, everybody!" he exclaimed softly. "Come look out the window."

The Rossos crowded around the front windows.

Standing at the feeder, his neck arched gracefully to reach the food inside, was a fawn.

"A deer baby!" said Jan. "Right?"

"Well, an old deer baby," Mr. Rosso replied. "He's already losing his spots. And you can see where his antlers are going to grow."

"He must be an orphan," said Faustine, "and he's having trouble finding food because of all the snow on the ground. Oh, Mom, can we adopt him?"

"No, we cannot," replied Mrs. Rosso. "No pets. Besides, honey, he's wild. He doesn't want to be adopted."

"Flag was adopted in *The Yearling*."

"But in the end, that didn't work out," said Mrs. Rosso. "Remember?"

Faustine nodded. But she and Hardy and the other kids wanted to adopt the fawn anyway. On Sunday, Mrs. Rosso agreed that they could put food out for it. Hardy, the twins, Jan, Ira, and Hannah tried to lure the fawn out of the woods, but he would only approach the food if no one was around.

"He can smell us, you know," Hardy told his brothers and sisters.

School opened again on Monday. The fawn ate in the morning while the Rosso kids were gone. He did the same thing on Tuesday and Wednesday. By Wednesday afternoon the snow was melting as the sun shone and the temperature rose. On Thursday the fawn did not return. The food that Hardy left for him remained untouched. The fawn didn't come back on Friday or Saturday either. He was gone.

"That's as it should be," said Mrs. Rosso.

"I guess," replied Hardy, but he was disappointed anyway. It would have been nice to have had a fawn for a pet.

# CHAPTER EIGHT
# *HANNAH*

Hannah Rosso sat in the secret room that Candy had found. She'd been going there a lot lately, more than any of the other kids. It was a pretty private place. Her parents still didn't know about it, and if she hung a washcloth on the inside knob of the closet door, the other kids took that as a sign not to enter the room.

Hannah was moping. She was moping for a lot of reasons. She was moping because her big mouth had gotten her into trouble in school again. She had merely *whispered* to someone that Nicole Barruch smelled, and her teacher had asked her to stay after school and then had told her that she would have extra homework that night. She was to write one hundred times, "I will not be unkind to others." How

119

had her teacher even heard what she'd said?

Furthermore, no one seemed to appreciate Hannah's practical jokes. At home her brothers and sisters just rolled their eyes. In school the other third-graders said things like "Hannah's being silly again" or "Hannah's acting like a baby again." They didn't think anything was funny, not even when Hannah left a dead spider on Nicole's desk and Nicole screamed.

The worst thing about Hannah's life, though, was her place in her family. She didn't fit in with anybody. She was too young for Abbie and Bainbridge and Candy. And everybody else had what Hannah thought of as a "special"—a brother or sister who was that person's favorite. Woody's special was Hardy and vice versa. The twins had each other (their specials were the best of all). And Jan and Ira were specials.

But Hannah had nobody. She was always too young or too old or not a boy. She hung around with Jan and Ira because she shared a room with them, but mostly she thought that *they* were too young for *her*. Well, Jan was, anyway. Ira was too neat.

So Hannah had been spending a lot of time in the secret room, reading Celia's diary. She wasn't a very good reader, and Celia's handwriting was messy and the ink had faded, but Hannah had read a number of parts. She'd covered the holidays first—Christmas, Thanksgiving, Easter, and Celia's birthday. (Hannah loved birthdays.) Then she'd read about summertime, and about starting school in the fall. She could easily identify with Celia, who wrote that she was often lonely. Hannah knew what it was like to be lonely with lots of people around. It was even worse than being lonely and alone.

After Hannah read about starting school, she realized that she'd forgotten to read about Valentine's Day. Did people even celebrate Valentine's Day way back when Celia was a girl? she wondered.

She turned to the beginning of February.

Yes. Celia was talking about Valentine cards. Hannah skipped ahead to find out where Celia bought hers. Hannah was going to buy hers at Hinkson's, which was in town, next door to Zinder's Dime Store. Hinkson's was a stationery store, and Hannah had thought they had very nice birthday cards. She'd bought a gorgeous one for her grandmother when Nanny had turned seventy. It had been the biggest card she could find. On the front was a lightly scented heart that said: Grandma. Inside were the words I Love You With All My Heart. Candy had said the card was inappropriate because they didn't call their grandmother Grandma, but Hannah knew that it was the thought that counted. And the thought here was that Hannah cared enough about Nanny to buy her the biggest birthday card in Hinkson's.

Hannah hadn't had a chance to look at Hinkson's valentines yet, and she was a little worried. What if

Hinkson's didn't carry the boxes of Peanuts valentines she'd always bought in New York? They were the best cards of all. They were funny, and they didn't cost too much, and you didn't have to punch them out or do anything to them except sign your name. And best of all, two boxes was enough for all of Hannah's classmates *and* her family.

Maybe Celia had bought Peanuts valentines, too. Hannah read carefully, but she couldn't find anything about going to town in early February. She turned back to January twenty-fifth and began reading from there. Finally, there it was—a trip into town to some-place called the Jersey General Store. But Celia didn't buy boxes of cards. She bought yards of ribbon and lace, some colored pencils, and some paper. Celia was going to *make* her valentines. Hannah was impressed until she realized that Celia probably didn't have to make twenty-six of them. That was how many Han-nah would need—twelve for the kids in her class, one for her teacher, nine for her brothers and sisters, one each for her parents, and one each for Nanny and Grandy, who would be visiting the Rossos on Valen-tine's Day.

Still . . . maybe Hannah could make her own valen-tines too. She could start right away and work in the secret room. It would be fun. There must be plenty of stuff to make cards with right in her house. After all, the Rossos had made their Christmas cards several months earlier.

Hannah began to feel excited. She ran downstairs and rooted around in the cabinets where Mrs. Rosso had stored the materials for card making and ornament making and decoration making. She found Magic Markers, paper, glue, scissors, glitter, scraps of lace and fabric, beads and buttons and doilies and sequins. Amazing!

With an armload of supplies teetering in front of her, Hannah returned to the secret room. She set to work immediately and decided to make the cards for her classmates first.

Hannah started by folding a piece of paper in half and making a beautiful rose on one side with red sequins and glitter. Then, with a grin, she wrote on the inside, "Roses are red, glue is sticky, Valentine's Day would be great if you weren't so icky." She disguised her handwriting by printing extra neatly, and she didn't sign her name. At the last minute she decided it would be more fun not to make cards for particular people but just to make them, hand them out, and see who got what. So she didn't bother to decide who the card was for either.

Over the next week Hannah spent all of her free time in the secret room making her valentines. She finished the cards for school and started on the ones for home. A brilliant idea came to her just as she was making the first card for her family. Maybe she could use the cards to hint to her parents how much she and her brothers and sisters wanted a dog. Hannah wouldn't sign these valentines either, so no one would know they were from her.

With a smile on her lips, Hannah began the first card. In a magazine she found a picture of a cocker spaniel, cut it out, and glued it to the front of the card. She made a border of colored stars and red hearts. Inside, in her best handwriting, Hannah printed, "Come snow or rain or wind or fog, we'd all be happier if we had a dog." Brilliant! Simply brilliant!

Hannah worked so hard that all of her cards were finished five days before Valentine's Day. The only things she needed to buy were envelopes for them. At Hinksons' she bought thirteen white ones and thirteen pink ones. Later she put the school cards in the white envelopes and the family cards in the pink ones. Most of them didn't fit very well, and she had to fold some of the edges in odd ways, but she didn't think that mattered much.

On Valentine's Day, Hannah woke up early. Her stomach was jittery with excitement. She loved receiving valentines, but this year she was also excited about giving out the special ones she had made. She couldn't wait to see what everyone thought about them. Best of all, they weren't signed. If no one liked them, they wouldn't know that it was Hannah who had made them.

Although Hannah had awakened early, she got behind schedule immediately. She wanted to look just right for the party at school that day, so she tried on several dresses before she found one she liked. Then she fussed with her hair and lost some more time looking for her gold heart locket.

"Come on, Hannah. Hurry up," Ira urged her.

Ira, of course, was perfectly dressed and ready for breakfast.

"I'm coming," said Hannah.

"You're going to be late."

"I *said* I'm coming."

Ira shrugged and left the room.

Hannah finished with her hair and found her locket. Then she ran downstairs and began breakfast. She was only about halfway done when Mrs. Rosso announced, "Five more minutes until the bus comes."

Hannah's brothers and sisters were through eating. They began to collect their lunches and books and put on their coats. Hannah quickly swallowed the toast that was in her mouth.

"Hannah, get a move on," said Mrs. Rosso.

"I'm almost ready." Hannah dashed upstairs. There was no time to brush her teeth. She pulled open her desk drawer, saw the two piles of envelopes and for a moment couldn't remember whether the pink ones or the white ones were for school. She should have written people's names on them, she thought, but it was too late for that now. Finally, she decided that the pink ones must be for school since they were prettier. She snatched them up and raced down the stairs.

"Have fun at your party, honey," Mrs. Rosso called to her as she ran out the door.

"I will!" Hannah called back. Then she hurried after her brothers and sisters who had already reached the end of the driveway.

Hannah's third-grade teacher was named Mrs. Pownell. Sometimes she and Hannah got along; sometimes they didn't. Hannah certainly wasn't the teacher's pet. She had played too many practical jokes and forgotten to raise her hand in class too many times. But Hannah liked math and science, and Mrs. Pownell always said nice things to her when she did well on her tests and assignments. So Hannah knew that Mrs. Pownell didn't hate her.

At the very beginning of the school year Mrs. Pownell had told Hannah's class that she especially liked Valentine's Day. Sure enough, during the past two weeks the class had made dozens of decorations for their room. They had studied about St. Valentine, and they had gone to the local historical society to see a display of old Valentine's Day cards.

Now—Hannah was sure of this—her class was

going to have the best Valentine party in the whole elementary school. The room mothers were bringing punch and cookies and cupcakes and heart-shaped candy. Mrs. Pownell was going to show her students how to play two games she'd made up called Love Notes and Heart Races. She was even going to give prizes to the winners. And after all *that* Hannah and her classmates would open their valentines.

Taped to the front of each desk in Mrs. Pownell's room was a paper mailbag. Hannah and her classmates had made them in art class. The bags were to hold the valentines that were delivered during the day.

Hannah couldn't wait to deliver hers, and she was glad to find that she was one of the first kids to arrive in her class that morning.

"Hi, Jane!" she cried. "Hi, Leigh!"

"Hi, Hannah. It's Valentine's Day!"

"I know. I can't wait for our party. I'm going to deliver my cards right now."

"Me too," said Jane and Leigh.

Hannah walked proudly around the room and dropped a pink envelope into each mailbag. She left the last one on Mrs. Pownell's desk. She was already so excited that her heart was thumping. How would she ever be able to wait for one fifteen when the party was to begin?

It wasn't easy, but of course Hannah did manage to

wait. And she called out of turn only twice and hid Randy Jamison's pencil once.

At one fifteen the room mothers arrived. They distributed punch and treats. Hannah could see Mrs. Pownell's game prizes on her desk. But what she really wanted to do was empty out her fat mailbag and open her valentines. All day long her classmates had been walking from desk to desk, dropping cards in the bags.

When the games were over, Mrs. Pownell said, "And now, class, you may open your valentines."

Hannah let out a whoop. She jumped up so fast that she knocked her chair over. But Mrs. Pownell didn't mind. Even she was reaching for her mailbag.

Hannah emptied her bag onto her desk. One, two, three . . . she counted the envelopes. Good. There were thirteen, one from every kid in the class and one from Mrs. Pownell.

She began to open them. She was on her third when she heard Jane say to somebody, "Hey, here's a weird one. It says, 'A cat, a gerbil, a mouse, a frog. Why can't we get just one little dog?'"

The poem sounded familiar, but Hannah was too busy to pay much attention to Jane. Not until Randy Jamison went prancing around the room singing, "Come snow or rain or wind or fog, we'd all be happier if we had a dog!" did she pay attention. Hannah had written that—hadn't she? But it was for her family. It was one of her pet hints. Uh-oh. . . .

Soon all the kids in Hannah's room were comparing the strange valentines with poems about pets.

"Who sent these?" asked Leigh. "They're not signed."

"Hey," said Jane, "Hannah's valentines were in pink envelopes. Did you send these, Hannah?"

"No," replied Hannah, blushing.

Jane frowned.

"Well," said Randy, looking suspiciously at Hannah, "did anyone get a card signed 'Hannah Rosso'?" Hannah wished she hadn't picked that day to tease Randy by hiding his pencil.

The kids checked through their valentines. "No!" they chorused.

"Hannah, these *are* your valentines!" exclaimed Jane. "How come they all say to get a dog or a cat or something?"

Hannah shrugged. She was trying to think of a good excuse when Dr. Moorehouse came into the classroom. Dr. Moorehouse was the principal of John Bowen Elementary. He was fat and pigeon-toed and always held on to the lapels of his coat when he was talking.

While he spoke with Mrs. Pownell, Hannah turned her back on the adults. She stuck her feet inward so that they pointed to each other, and she placed her hands on her dress as if she were holding onto lapels.

Then she pretended to have a conversation with someone.

"Mrmph, mrmph, mrmph," she said, which was how Dr. Moorehouse sounded when he tried to whisper.

Jane and Leigh began to giggle. So did Randy. So did everyone who could see Hannah. And then the bell rang. The party was over, and Hannah's valentines were forgotten.

But Hannah still had a problem. She worried about it all the way home on the bus. The problem was her other valentines, the ones in the white envelopes. They had been made for her classmates, and some of them were . . . well, it wasn't that they were mean exactly, but Hannah really didn't want to give her grandmother a card that said, "Roses are red, glue is sticky, Valentine's Day would be great if you weren't so icky."

When the bus stopped at the end of the Rossos' driveway, Hannah jumped off. She followed Jan, Ira, the twins, and Hardy to the house. She was busy thinking. What should she do? What *could* she do?

Hannah didn't bother to eat a snack. She took off her coat and went straight upstairs to her room. Mrs. Rosso watched her worriedly. In her room Hannah left her reading book on her bed. She removed the stack of white envelopes from the desk drawer and took them into the secret room with her. She sat on the floor.

"Oh, Celia," she murmured. "What am I going to do now? I can't give these cards to my family. I don't have enough money to buy cards, and I don't have enough time to make new ones." And then she thought, Boy, all that hard work for nothing. Her pet hints had been wasted.

Nanny and Grandy, Mr. Rosso's parents, were coming over for dinner at five o'clock. Hannah looked at her watch. She had only an hour and a half in which to do something. Once her grandparents arrived, she'd be busy with them, with dinner . . . and then opening more cards.

Hannah thought and thought. At last, an idea came to her. It just might work. It was something she could do quickly that would take the place of valentines very nicely. Only this time Hannah would be smart. She'd write names on the envelopes and sign her notes. Hannah found a pen and some paper and got to work.

Nanny and Grandy arrived promptly at five o'clock. Hannah loved her grandparents' visits. When she heard a knock, she, Jan, Ira, Woody, and Candy stampeded to the back door.

"Hello, hello!" called Grandy.

He and Nanny stepped inside, stomping snow off their boots and rubbing their hands together.

"How are all my chickens?" asked Nanny.

"We're fine," replied Hannah, who never minded that Nanny called her her chicken. But if anyone *else* had ever called her that . . .

Grandy was tall and heavy and ruddy-cheeked, and Nanny was tiny and thin and roselike. They loved the Rosso kids, and Hannah and her brothers and sisters loved them back.

Nanny and Grandy never arrived at the Rossos' empty-handed, but Jan was the only one young enough to ask, "What did you bring us?" She jumped up and down.

Nanny produced a shopping bag, and the kids peered inside. Hannah saw cards, naturally, and a pile of red-wrapped gifts. "But they're for later," Nanny cautioned. "They go with dessert."

Despite her disappointment over the mix-up with her own cards, Hannah could feel excitement returning. Mrs. Rosso was preparing a turkey dinner, and —who knew?—maybe there would be even more presents.

When Abbie and Bainbridge added every leaf to the dining room table, fourteen Rossos could just barely squeeze around it. They ate roast turkey and mashed potatoes and peas by candlelight.

"I know what dessert is!" Jan kept saying, and finally it was time to produce the dessert—a white sheet cake decorated with red candy hearts. Hannah thought she had eaten enough cake and candy in school that day to last a year, but now she wasn't sure.

Mr. Rosso served the cake, and Mrs. Rosso poured coffee for the adults, and Jan kept asking, "Is it time? Is it time?"

At long last, Mrs. Rosso replied, "Yes."

There was a scramble as the Rossos reached under their chairs for their Valentine's Day cards and gifts and passed them out. When they had finished, Hannah found herself facing a pile of envelopes for the second time that day—and two presents. She opened the presents first. In Nanny's red box was a tiny gold heart to pin on her dress. In a box from her parents were heart-shaped barrettes.

"Hey, Hannah! Neat!" exclaimed Hardy suddenly. "Thanks." He held up the Valentine from Hannah— a slip of paper that read "I.O.U. one week of bed-making. Love, Hannah."

"Look at this!" exclaimed Faustine. "'I.O.U. one week of braided hair.' You're going to braid my hair for a week, Hannah? Great!"

Everyone began searching for their I.O.U.'s from Hannah. Her last-minute valentines were a hit. Hannah beamed. She had squeaked through this mess okay. But she'd be doing favors forever. And her pet reminders had gone to the wrong people.

Oh well, thought Hannah, I'll save my pet hints for Christmas cards.

# CHAPTER NINE
# *FAUSTINE*

One Saturday in April the temperature rose to sixty-five degrees.

"It's spring!" cried Faustine. "All of a sudden, spring is here."

"And it's the weekend," added Dinnie. "Rimbald tango." (Extra specially good.)

It certainly did seem like spring. On the Rosso farm Faustine could smell spring, see spring, hear spring, and feel spring. It was everywhere. It was in the tinge of green on the trees and bushes, the blush of pink on the dogwoods and magnolias, the fuzz of yellow on the forsythia. It was in the Rossos' very own brook, which rushed along noisily, still swollen with runoff from the winter's snow. It was in the newly warm air, which smelled of grass and leaves and other green, living things. It was in the robins and sparrows and wrens and cardinals and chicka- dees, which had become very busy building nests and raising families.

Faustine especially liked the birds. She didn't re- member birds in New York, except for sparrows and pigeons. The pigeons had been brash and pushy and uppity. They'd fought over all kinds of things that birds had no business eating in the first place, such as pizza and the ends of hot dogs. But on the New Jer- sey farm, there wasn't a single pigeon to be seen.

In March, Faustine had announced, "I saw a robin today!"

"Must have been the first robin, bringing spring," her father had told her.

"What?"

"The first robin that you see brings spring. Watch now. Spring won't be far off," Mr. Rosso said. Then he'd returned to a carpentry magazine.

He'd been right. Very slowly, spring had crept up on the farm. It had settled over it like a fresh, warm blanket, and on that day in April, a month later, Faustine was sure it was through arriving.

"Sixty-five degrees is almost summer," she said. She and Dinnie had run outside barefoot with their sweat shirts tied around their waists. They planned to go wading in the brook.

But Mrs. Rosso called them back. "Shoes," she said, pointing to their feet.

"Mom, it's sixty-five degrees today," Faustine pointed out.

"It's the middle of April," Mrs. Rosso countered. "It's not *that* warm. And the brook will be freezing, even if the air isn't. Put on socks and shoes and your sweat shirts. And no wading."

The twins had obeyed unhappily. "Moochie salamin," they had grumbled.

But the day was too nice to let socks and shoes and sweat shirts get in the way. And there were plenty of other things to do besides wading in the brook (which *was* freezing).

They walked through the woods, and after awhile they were glad they were wearing their sweat shirts. Dinnie had brought a book about wild flowers with her, and Faustine had brought a book about birds. In their pockets were pads of paper and pencils. Faustine's pad was labeled "Birds." Dinnie's was labeled "Flowers." They planned to make lists of the birds and flowers they saw.

"Hey, what's this?" asked Dinnie, pausing by some small purple blooms clustered at the roots of a sycamore tree.

"Bluebells?" Faustine suggested.

Dinnie shook her head. "Bluebells were last month." She opened her book. "Oh, they're violets!"

she exclaimed. She wrote "violets" on her list.

As the morning wore on, they added lilies, grape hyacinths, and jonquils to Dinnie's list. Faustine's list was longer. The twins spotted all sorts of birds—a mud-colored female cardinal, another robin, several sparrows, a blackbird, a crow, and even a hawk soaring overhead. Once Faustine thought she saw a hummingbird, but it turned out to be a large flying insect, which was disappointing.

Nevertheless, they sat down under an oak tree to examine the insect. When it had flown away, Dinnie said, "We should have brought lunches with us. We could have eaten them right here, just as if we were real nature explorers."

She was answered by a harsh squawk and looked at her twin suspiciously.

"That wasn't me," said Faustine. "It came from around the tree."

"From around the tree?" Dinnie's eyes met Faustine's nervously.

Faustine stretched out her fingers until they touched Dinnie's. The twins clasped hands desperately.

"What do you suppose is back there?" Dinnie whispered.

"A snark-blandit?"

"Don't be silly," replied Dinnie. "We made up snark-blandits." But she didn't look very convinced.

*Squawk.* The cry came again.

"Eeee!" shrieked Faustine. She and Dinnie clutched hands more tightly and leaped to their feet.

*Squawk, squawk, squawk.*

"Whatever it is, it sounds kind of scared," Faustine whispered.

"Well, we'll just have to peek around the tree," said Dinnie.

The twins peered around one side of the tree. They leaned over farther and farther.

"I don't see anything," said Dinnie.

"Look down," Faustine told her.

Dinnie looked at the base of the tree, and her eyes discovered what Faustine's had already found.

It was a grackle, a large blackbird with iridescent feathers and a long tail. It sounded very unhappy.

Faustine knelt beside the grackle. "Aw, it's hurt," she cried softly. "Dinnie, its wing is hurt."

The twins crouched beside the bird. It stared at them with beady eyes. When Faustine stroked one of its wings, it let out another squawk and struggled away awkwardly, one wing flapping, the other barely moving.

"I think its wing is broken!" Faustine exclaimed.

"We better take it home with us," said Dinnie.

"Oh," said Faustine, "Mom'll never let us keep a bird."

"Yes, she will. She'll let us have an injured one. We have to make it well. She can't say no to a bird with a broken wing. That would be cruel."

"She can too say no," replied Faustine. But she knew that she could never leave the bird lying in the woods. She and Dinnie would have to try to convince their mother that it was all right to keep the bird. At least until it was well.

Dinnie was looking at Faustine expectantly. "Okay," said Faustine. "Let's go. But how are we going to get it home?"

"In my sweat shirt," said Dinnie immediately. She peeled off her sweat shirt and wrapped it around the bird.

The grackle squawked. Goosebumps rose on Dinnie's arms because the woods were shady and cool. But the twins marched resolutely back to the farm.

"I'll talk to Mom," said Faustine on the way. "She still mentions Goliath, and Goliath was your, um, mistake, so she's not going to be too happy if you bring her another bird."

"Okay," agreed Dinnie, her face reddening. Under her breath she muttered, "Moochie salamin."

When the twins returned to the farmyard, Dinnie handed Faustine the bird. They hadn't even reached the house when Mrs. Rosso called from the back door, "Gardenia, where is your sweat shirt?"

"It's right here," Faustine replied for Dinnie, pointing. "Mom, we found a bird with a broken wing."

Mrs. Rosso stepped outside and peered into the depths of Dinnie's sweat shirt. "Oh, girls," she groaned.

"We know how you feel about pets," said Faustine, "but all we want to do is make the bird well."

"What's that?" asked Bainbridge, striding out the back door.

Dinnie showed him. "Can you help us set the wing?" she asked.

Bainbridge looked at his mother with raised eyebrows.

Mrs. Rosso sighed. "Oh, go ahead," she said, waving the bird away. She marched back into the house.

The twins giggled. "Groode!" exclaimed Dinnie.

"Bainbridge, do you know how to set the wing?" asked Faustine.

"Uh . . . sure," he replied. "I've seen it done on TV. We'll make a splint for it out of popsicle sticks, and then bind the wing to the body. We'll let him—or her—use the other wing. . . . I wonder if this is a girl or a boy."

A half hour later the bird was settled into the corner of a carton that had once held cans of condensed milk. Its wing was set and bandaged. It had squawked horribly during the procedure but now was quiet.

Bainbridge looked very proud of himself. "Maybe I'll become a vet," he said importantly.

Faustine managed to persuade her mother to let the bird stay in the twins' room. "See how quiet it is now? It won't be any trouble."

She and Dinnie lined the box with rags and put a dish of water and some leaves and grass and birdseed and even an insect in the box. They weren't sure what grackles ate, but they thought the birdseed should do for a few days. All birds ate birdseed, didn't they?

Then they decided to name the bird. "Let's pick the plainest, nicest name we know," said Faustine, rocking back on her heels and looking at her sister.

"Girl's name or boy's name?" asked Dinnie.

"Girl's. I think it's a girl, don't you?"

Dinnie nodded. "How about Patricia?"

"That's not plain. How about Cynthia?"

"That's not plain either."

The twins considered Jennifer, Sarah, Emily, and Mandy and finally decided on Sally.

"Plainest of plain," said Faustine.

By bedtime that night, all of the Rosso kids had spent time in the twins' room, leaning over the box and cooing at Sally, or talking to her, or trying to stroke the top of her shiny head.

"She's awful quiet," Hannah observed.

"I think she's had too much excitement," said Faustine. "We should leave her alone for awhile."

"Right," said Dinnie. "She hasn't eaten a thing. She hasn't even moved out of that corner."

The twins were worried about Sally, but neither wanted to admit it. Instead they asked Hannah to leave the room. Then Dinnie hung a No Visitors sign on the bedroom door.

"I think we should check on Sally all night," said Faustine as she and Dinnie were putting their pajamas on.

"Okay," agreed Dinnie.

"Let's see. It's nine thirty now. I'll check on her at midnight, you check on her at three, and I'll check on her again at six."

That was the plan, and the twins stuck to it nicely at first. When the alarm went off at midnight, Faustine looked in on Sally, who appeared to be sleeping. She moved some of the bird seed closer to her. Sally stirred, but didn't try to eat it. Faustine reset the alarm for three. At three o'clock Dinnie sleepily peered in at Sally and offered her some water, but Sally wasn't interested. Dinnie reset the alarm for six. At six o'clock Faustine turned off the alarm, but she didn't get out of bed. She just couldn't. She was much too tired. "I'll see you when we get up," she murmured to Sally from the coziness of her covers. "I hope you feel better then."

But when the twins arose at eight thirty, Sally was dead. She was lying stiffly on her side in the corner of the condensed milk box.

"Oh, no!" cried Faustine. "This is all my fault! I should have checked on her at six, but instead I went back to sleep. It's my fault for being lazy. Now we don't even have an injured pet."

Dinnie didn't say anything. She couldn't help thinking that her sister was right.

But Mrs. Rosso had a different opinion. "I think Sally might have died no matter what. We don't know how she broke her wing. Maybe she had other injuries too. You girls did the very best you could."

Faustine felt only a tiny bit better.

It was Ira who suggested holding a funeral for Sally.

"A funeral," repeated Faustine thoughtfully. Maybe she would feel better after a funeral.

The other kids liked the idea, and they began to make plans.


Sally's funeral began at two o'clock that afternoon. In preparation Faustine had fixed up a shoe box and placed Sally in it, splint and all, and Bainbridge had dug a shoe-box-size hole in the ground near the oak tree, behind the house.

The Rossos gathered there, and Bainbridge placed

the box in the hole while Woody played his harmonica. He had to play "Home on the Range" because that was the only song he knew.

Then Faustine and Dinnie delivered the eulogy. They each said some kind things about Sally. Their eulogy was very nice, except that it was constantly interrupted by loud cheeping from somewhere nearby.

"Be quiet, you birds," Ira hissed. He wanted Sally's funeral to be perfect.

The cheeping continued as Bainbridge buried the shoe box and Dinnie placed a rock on the spot as a gravestone.

"Birds! Shh!" Ira commanded.

It continued while Faustine placed a bunch of violets next to the gravestone. Then the funeral was over.

"What *is* all that noise?" exclaimed Abbie.

"Let's go see," said Jan. She was already heading for a nearby tree, a low one with lots of branches, and she began to climb up.

"Are you sure the noise is coming from that tree?" asked Hannah.

"Yup," replied Jan. And she was right. "Ooh," she said softly, a few moments later. "Look what I found."

"What?" cried the others from below.

"Bird babies. A whole nest of them."

"Well, come down right now," Faustine ordered.

"If the mother comes back and smells a human, she won't go near her babies."

"Really?" asked Jan, astonished. She climbed out of the tree as fast as she could, jumping the last few feet to the ground.

The Rossos found a spot several yards away where they could see the nest, and they stood there for over an hour, waiting for the mother to return and feed them.

But no bird even flew near to the tree. The cheeping became more insistent.

Hardy ran inside and found a pair of binoculars and a pair of opera glasses. The watching continued, but no mother (or father) appeared.

"Maybe Sally was their mother!" Jan exclaimed.

"Maybe," said Faustine, "but I don't think so. We found her awfully far away from here. And we've had her for an entire day now. Twenty-four hours. I don't think the babies could go that long without food."

By suppertime no big bird had arrived at the nest, and the cheeping was quieting down.

"It sounds like the babies have given up," said Ira sadly.

Even Mrs. Rosso seemed concerned about the baby birds. "I do think we ought to do something about them," she said while they were eating dinner. "I'd hate to see them die."

A window was open in the dining room, and every

now and then a feeble chirp could be heard.

"Baby birds need to eat all the time," Dinnie pointed out.

The Rossos held a discussion, and Mr. Rosso was elected to phone Mr. Pritchard and find out what vet he used. Then Faustine was elected to phone the vet, Dr. Benardi, and find out what to do for the birds.

An hour later the nest, babies and all, had been taken out of the tree and placed in a big box lined with rags. Abbie, Candy, Dinnie, and Faustine were each feeding one of the four baby birds with an eye dropper. The babies were going to need frequent feedings, and the Rossos had worked out a schedule that allowed two of them to be up with the babies every hour that night. Even Mrs. Rosso was going to help with the feedings, although she said more than once, "I thought I was finished with two o'clock feedings after Janthina outgrew them."

The next morning Faustine woke up groggily. She'd gotten up twice during the night to feed the birds. The second time, which had been at five a.m., the birds had eaten hungrily and chirped excitedly. Even so, Faustine couldn't help being afraid that she would now find the babies dead, as she had found Sally dead the day before.

But when she tiptoed into the den, where the heat had been turned up for the birds' sake, she found her mother bent over the box with an eyedropper, and four eager beaks opening and closing.

"Oh, they're all alive," whispered Faustine.

"Very much so," replied Mrs. Rosso with a smile.

Over the next few weeks the birds grew rapidly. They were not, as it turned out, Sally's babies, since they were sparrows, not grackles. Much of the feeding of the birds fell to Mrs. Rosso, who was the only one at home during school days, but Faustine and her brothers and sisters took over whenever they could. They were glad to see Mrs. Rosso pitching in, though. She actually seemed to like caring for the birds.

"Maybe, when they're all grown up, we can keep them," Faustine said hopefully to Dinnie one day.

"Or at least one of them," Dinnie replied.

But that conversation took place before the babies began learning to fly. Until then they had stayed safely in the box (the nest was gone), hopping from corner to corner and side to side, with no danger of getting out. The Rossos didn't even have to cover the box.

Then one day Candy was playing with the birds, and she perched one on the edge of the carton. To her surprise it fluttered its wings and flopped to the floor outside the box. After that, whenever one of the birds was anywhere above ground, it tried out its wings. None of the babies had much success at first, but they were getting better, and finally the Rossos had to cover the box with a screen if they weren't going to be near the birds.

As the weather grew even warmer, Faustine and Dinnie began carrying the box outside after school. Then they would take the babies out one by one to play in the farmyard.

"Remember what Dr. Benardi said to do next," Faustine reminded her sister.

"Right. The babies have to learn to find their own food."

The babies had no trouble with this. They were much better than the girls at spotting insects and grubs. Just in case, though, the twins showed them where the bird feeder was.

Finally, it became difficult to contain the birds in their box. "They're getting to be champion flyers," said Faustine, feeling both proud and sad. And at last came the day when Mrs. Rosso announced: "It's time to set the birds free."

"All of them?" asked Faustine.

"Yes, all of them," replied her mother firmly.

"Couldn't we keep just one?"

It was breakfast time on a Saturday morning, and Faustine looked pleadingly at her brothers and sisters, who in turn looked pleadingly at both of their parents.

"Kids," said Mr. Rosso, "the birds are wild things, just like the fawn was. They deserve their freedom."

So that morning, the bird box was carried outdoors for the last time, and, one by one, the babies were tossed into the air. Each flew steadily to a nearby tree.

"Good-bye, birds," whispered Faustine.

For a long time afterward, whenever she saw a sparrow on the property, Faustine wondered if it was one of "hers." Maybe next year, she thought, Mom will change her mind and let us keep a bird.

# CHAPTER TEN
# *BAINBRIDGE*

Bainbridge could hardly believe that summer vacation had finally arrived. He loved summertime, and he'd been looking forward to the end of school for months, but what, he wondered, would he and his brothers and sisters do on the farm for seventy-four days, which was exactly how long summer vacation would last?

In the beginning they had found plenty of things to do—all the things they hadn't had enough time for while they were in school. But after two weeks they'd had their fill of exploring and catching up on soap operas and playing statue outdoors in the cool gray twilight that followed supper.

For the first time ever, they began to feel isolated on their farm.

"I wish we could get ice-cream cones somewhere," said Jan one day. "Remember in New York? We could walk right to Safari Sundae, and sometimes Mr. Softee would drive by."

"I wish we could go to Bloomingdale's and shop for summer clothes," said Abbie wistfully.

"I wish we could go to the Last Wound-Up for those great wind-up toys," added Woody.

They didn't even get to go into the little town very often because Mrs. Rosso hadn't been feeling well lately. Once Bainbridge had ridden to the town on his bicycle, but it had taken forever, and he'd sworn he wouldn't do it again.

Every time Bainbridge or one of the other kids asked about a trip into town, their mother complained that the summer heat was making her too tired. She began ordering groceries over the phone and having them delivered to the farm, even though that was more expensive. And she spent most of every day lying on the couch in the living room with a cloth over her eyes. She couldn't eat a thing.

"Must be the flu," said Bainbridge slowly, but he was more worried than he let on.

After a week of boredom Bainbridge became bored with being bored and decided to do something about it. His all-time favorite occupation was football, but he hadn't had much opportunity to play since he'd moved to the farm. The middle school didn't have a team, and he could rarely get enough friends together after school for a scrimmage. There was a league in town, but how many of the farm kids could get all the way into town for practice several times a week?

"So I'm going to start my own team," Bainbridge told Mrs. Rosso while keeping her company in the living room one day.

"Your own team?" Mrs. Rosso repeated. Her eyes were covered with a damp cloth as usual, and her face was pale.

"Yeah," replied Bainbridge. "With all us farm kids out here. Getting together won't be easy, but it'll be easier than going into town. And there are a bunch of kids who'd be interested, I think. When we're organized, maybe we can play the town league sometimes. At least we can keep in shape for football tryouts at high school this fall."

"That sounds good. . . . Who would you ask to join?" Mrs. Rosso was lying very still. She said she felt seasick and that any little motion would upset her. Bainbridge was sitting on the floor across the room so as not to bother her.

"Well, there are about five boys from my grade," he said. "And Mr. Pritchard's grandson. He's a year behind me. He lives down the road, next to the Pritchards. And Dana Benardi—he's the vet's son."

"Mmm," murmured Mrs. Rosso. "Bainbridge, are

you eating something? I smell...I don't know...
cauliflower or peanuts or something."

"No, Mom, honest. I'm not eating. I don't think
anyone is, but I'll see if someone left food out in the
kitchen."

Bainbridge rushed into the kitchen. He found an
open jar of peanut butter, which he capped and put
away. Food smells—almost any smell, for that matter—drove his mother wild these days.

He returned to the living room. "It was peanut
butter, Mom," he announced. "But I put it away."

"Oh, thank you," said Mrs. Rosso with a groan.
"Peanut butter. Ugh."

At that moment Jan strolled through the living
room with a gigantic, gloppy peanut butter and mayonnaise sandwich.

"Oh," cried Mrs. Rosso. "There's that awful smell
again!"

"Jan, get that out of here!" exclaimed Bainbridge.

But it was too late. His mother was already running for the bathroom.

Bainbridge did just what he'd told his mother he
was going to do. Early the next morning, he hopped
on his ten-speed bicycle and rode to Doug Pritchard's
farm. He found Doug and his father, who was old
Mr. Pritchard's son, sprawled under a tractor, surrounded by tools and greasy cloths.

"Hey, Doug!" Bainbridge called, hopping expertly off his bike.

"Hey!" Doug replied, grinning. He wiped his hands on his jeans, which were as greasy as the cloths, and got to his feet. "Dad?" he said. "This is Bainbridge Rosso. You know, one of *the* Rossos."

Bainbridge was used to such introductions.

"Pleased to meet you," said Mr. Pritchard, sounding muffled under the tractor. "I hope you'll excuse me if I don't—oof—get up."

"That's okay," said Bainbridge.

"So what have you been doing this summer?" asked Doug.

"Getting bored mostly," replied Bainbridge. "There's not much to do on our farm." He gazed around at Doug Pritchard's farm—a working farm— and saw just how much needed to be done. There was machinery to be repaired, and there were animals to be fed, crops to be tended, and a house and two barns to be cared for. A funny feeling crept into his stomach. How was someone like Doug going to have time for football? This farm was more than a job; it was his life. Bainbridge sensed that immediately.

He shifted from one foot to the other. "I guess you're pretty busy all summer," he ventured. "With the farm and all."

"Yeah, pretty busy," Doug agreed. "Hey, is something wrong?"

"No, no," replied Bainbridge quickly. "I had an idea, but I don't think it was a very good one. Doesn't matter, though."

"What was the idea?" asked Doug. "You gotta tell me. Don't leave me hanging."

"We-ell," said Bainbridge slowly, "I wanted to start a football team out here—you know, for all us farm kids."

Mr. Pritchard poked his head out from under the tractor. "Now I think that's a great idea," he said. "Doug spends too much time stuck on the farm during the summer. He never sees his friends. If football practice wouldn't take up too much time, I'd be all for it."

"Really?" said Doug and Bainbridge at the same time.

"Sure. But you have to get a sponsor if you want to be a real team. Did you know that? I mean, if you want uniforms and want to play the town league from time to time."

"A sponsor?" repeated Bainbridge. "What do you mean?"

"I mean, for instance, a business from town. How it works is, say, Zinder's buys uniforms for your team and pays for expenses, and in return your team is free good publicity for them. Your team name would be the Zinder's Bombers or something, and your uniforms would say 'Zinder's' on them. . . . You'd need a coach, too," added Doug's father.

"Gosh," said Bainbridge, "I didn't know it would be so complicated."

"Before you look for a sponsor, you better get a team together, though."

"That's true. You want to come with me, Doug?"

"I can't," Doug replied. "Not today. We have to finish with this tractor. And then I've got some work to do in the barn. Maybe tomorrow."

"Okay," agreed Bainbridge. "I'll call you tonight and let you know how I'm doing."

Bainbridge's next stop was Dana Benardi's. He figured Dana would be an easy catch since the Benardis lived on a farm that, like the Rossos', wasn't a working farm. Dr. Benardi was the vet, and the Benardis simply liked country living. However, Bainbridge noted as he walked his bicycle up the gravel driveway, the Benardis did have some pets. He saw a horse, a German shepherd, and two kittens before he saw Dana himself.

Dana was standing over a ten-speed bicycle that was balanced upside down by the driveway. A box of tools was open at his feet, and he was spinning tires and checking gears.

"Problems?" Bainbridge called when he was several yards away. He didn't know Dana well and was glad for the broken bicycle. It would give them something to talk about.

"Hi, Bainbridge," said Dana, looking surprised. "Yeah. Something's wrong with the brakes. They keep slipping."

Bainbridge parked his own bike and stooped down to examine Dana's. They worked on it together for several minutes. When they stood up, their hands were black with grease, but the bicycle was working.

"What are you up to this summer?" asked Dana after he had thanked Bainbridge.

"Not much," replied Bainbridge. "What are you up to?"

"Not much." Dana grinned. "I help my dad sometimes, and I do a little work around the farm, but . . ." Dana shrugged as if to say, "You know how boring things can get."

Bainbridge nodded.

"I wish I could get a job," Dana went on, "but my mom won't let me do that until I'm fifteen."

"Well, I know something you can do," Bainbridge said. "That's why I'm here." He explained his idea about a "farm" football league. Then he told him what Doug Pritchard's father had said. "You want to help me with the team?" he asked finally.

"Sure!" said Dana. "That's fantastic. I think we could really do it."

"I hope so," replied Bainbridge. "It isn't going to be easy."

Doug and Bainbridge worked hard that day. They

rode to six other farms to talk to kids they knew. Everyone was interested but admitted that they didn't have much time. By late in the afternoon Bainbridge had had enough for one day, and he and Dana agreed to meet again the next morning.

Bainbridge rode home, zipping along the country roads, smelling leaves and dust and honeysuckle and watching the mottled sunlight on his arms as it filtered through the trees.

At home Bainbridge found his mother feeling better. At least he assumed she was because she was on her feet in the kitchen making dinner. There were all sorts of smelly things around her—hot dogs and mayonnaise and lemons and horseradish—and she didn't even look green.

"Mom!" he exclaimed. "What are you doing? Are you okay?"

"I'm feeling much better, thanks," she replied. "And in celebration, I'm making us a picnic supper. We'll have hot dogs and hamburgers and potato salad, and we'll eat outdoors at the wooden table."

"You're going to *eat?*" asked Bainbridge, amazed.

"I certainly am," replied his mother. "Now, could you round up some of your brothers and sisters? I need a little help here."

Later, after dinner was over, Bainbridge realized that the picnic was a meal he would never forget. Not that it had been spectacular, since hot dogs and hamburgers seem ordinary no matter what you do to them. It was what happened during the meal.

The twelve Rossos had sat down to a later-than-usual dinner. They'd waited for Mr. Rosso to come home from New York, and then the barbecue had taken longer to start than anyone had expected. (It always took longer than expected, but nobody ever expected *that*.)

By seven thirty, though, the picnic table had been set, and a plate of hot dogs and hamburgers sat at one end. Mrs. Rosso asked the kids to seat themselves in alphabetical order, so Abbie, Bainbridge, Candy, Woody, and Hardy sat opposite Faustine, Dinnie, Hannah, Ira, and Jan. Mr. and Mrs. Rosso each sat at an end.

For the next few minutes food was passed back and forth, and nobody spoke except to say things like, "Jan, you've got ketchup on your elbow" or "Isn't there any horseradish?" or "Hardy, you are such a *pig!*" (that was Woody). Then Hannah spilled her milk and, in trying to mop it up, spilled Mr. Rosso's iced tea too.

At last everyone was served and ready to eat. Bainbridge was just thinking that his mother still looked awfully tired, when suddenly she stood up. "I have an announcement to make," she said.

She smiled the way you do when you feel like

laughing and crying at the same time. Something *emotional* or very exciting must have happened, thought Bainbridge, and he grew nervous. He set his hamburger on his plate, put his hands in his lap, and waited. Up and down the benches on either side of the table nine other Rossos were waiting, too. Mr. Rosso was grinning.

"As you know," began Mrs. Rosso, "our family seems just right to me. I always wanted to have ten children, each a year apart, and that's what your father and I did."

"Except for us," chimed in Dinnie.

"Except for you," agreed Mrs. Rosso, "but I'd rather have twins than perfect stairsteps."

The twins looked at each other and smiled.

"Well," their mother went on, "although we hadn't planned this, it seems that our family is going to increase by one member—"

"A dog! A dog!" Jan shrieked. "We're getting a dog after all! Oh, I knew we would!" She jumped up and ran to her mother.

"I'm glad we saved the food dish and toys and stuff," Hannah whispered, leaning across the table to Woody.

"Jan, kids, I'm sorry to disappoint you," said Mrs. Rosso, disentangling Jan from her legs and aiming her toward her place at the table. "We're not getting a dog. . . . I'm pregnant. I'm going to have another baby."

Bainbridge and his brothers and sisters were slow to react.

"Another baby?" Candy repeated.

"Eleven kids," Ira said under his breath.

The twins stared at each other. "Inmooglay!" exclaimed Dinnie.

Bainbridge's mouth dropped down.

Hardy's fork clattered onto the table.

"No dog?" Jan cried.

Then Abbie jumped up, ran to the other end of the table, and hugged her mother. "Oh, Mom! That's wonderful!" she exclaimed.

Hardy retrieved his fork and kissed Mrs. Rosso.

Suddenly all of the kids were exclaiming, "A baby! Oh, wow!" and "I can't believe it!" and "I hope it's another girl," and "*I* hope it's another boy."

Bainbridge hugged his father.

Hannah leaned across Ira and said to Jan, "Hey, squirt, now you won't be the baby of the family anymore."

Jan burst into tears.

"Hannah, why did you have to say *that?*" asked Ira. "That was mean." He put one arm protectively across Jan's shoulders, and Jan stuck her tongue out at Hannah, who stuck *her* tongue out at both Jan and Ira.

Suddenly Bainbridge thought of something. As the oldest boy in the family, he would ordinarily have kept quiet and discussed his idea with his parents in private. But in all the excitement he couldn't help himself.

"Hey, Mom, Dad," said Bainbridge in a tone of voice that made everyone quiet down and look at him. "You've always said we can't get a pet because ten kids is enough. But now you guys are having another kid, so I think *we* ought to be able to have a dog—or something."

Mr. and Mrs. Rosso looked at each other down the length of the picnic table. Mr. Rosso raised his eyebrows questioningly.

But Mrs. Rosso's only response was, "Ten kids is enough."

"Not fair," said Faustine flatly.

"No way," agreed Hardy.

"A rule is a rule," Mrs. Rosso persisted.

"You broke the rule," Abbie pointed out patiently. "You said ten kids is enough, and now you're going to have eleven kids. If you get to have one more, why can't we have a pet?"

"Because—"

"And don't say, 'Because I said so,'" said Woody.

Bainbridge shot Woody a withering look. Now was not the time to be rude, no matter how unfair their mother was being.

"Young man," Mr. Rosso began warningly.

"Sorry," Woody apologized quickly.

"How come, Mom?" Jan asked.

"Because I know who would end up feeding the pet and cleaning up after it and training it and exercising it."

"We would," said Candy quietly.

"But if you didn't, I'd have a new baby *and* a pet to care for," Mrs. Rosso pointed out.

"Mom?" spoke up Ira. "What if you made a rule about the pet?"

Everyone looked at Ira questioningly.

"What, honey?" said Mrs. Rosso.

"You make lots of rules, and we follow them all, don't we?"

Bainbridge suddenly understood what his little brother was trying to say. "Yeah. We always put the folded clothes on the bottom of the piles, and we sit in the van in alphabetical order."

"So make up a rule about a pet," Ira went on. "Like, on even-numbered days kids A through E take care of the pet. On odd-numbered days kids F through J take care of it."

"Hey! No way!" cried Hardy. "Ira, you little sneak. There are more odd-numbered days than even-numbered ones."

"See what I mean?" said Mrs. Rosso. "It's already starting."

But Hardy didn't hear her. "The F-through-J kids would get to take care of the pet more than the rest of us would," he said crossly.

There was a moment of silence. Then everyone began to laugh.

"Mom?" Bainbridge asked again. "Our pet?"

"I'll think about it," his mother replied, still smiling.

"I'll help her," Mr. Rosso added.

Mrs. Rosso didn't give the kids an answer until the next day.

Her answer was yes.

That night the ten Rosso kids held a meeting in the boys' bedroom.

"Any kind of pet we want!" Hardy was saying. "So of course we'll get a dog."

"Of course," agreed the others.

"Where's the best pet store?" Candy wondered.

"Who cares?" said Woody. "Let's decide what kind of dog to get. I want a Doberman pinscher."

"I want a cocker spaniel," said Abbie.

"I want a beagle," said Ira. "Like Snoopy."

"I want a collie," said Jan. "Like Lassie."

"I want a Welsh corgi," said Candy.

"I want a golden retriever," said Hardy.

"I want a poodle," said Dinnie.

"I want a toy poodle," said Faustine.

"I want a Saint Bernard," said Hannah.

"I want a Great Dane," said Bainbridge.

"Well, now what?" asked Woody.

"Maybe," said Dinnie, "instead of deciding what kind of dog to get, we should just go to the pound and see what they have."

"The pound!" exclaimed Woody.

"Yes," replied Dinnie. "Give a home to a dog without a home."

"Right," agreed Faustine.

"You know," said Bainbridge, "I think that's the only thing to do. Does everyone agree?"

Everyone agreed, except for Woody, who had his heart set on a Doberman pinscher.

"Woody," said Bainbridge, "Mom and Dad said we could get a dog, not a monster. I don't think they'd okay a Doberman pinscher anyway."

Woody nodded his head in resignation. He didn't look happy.

"Hey!" exclaimed Abbie. "Let's get *What Shall We Name the Baby?* and figure out what the new baby will be named! Oh, I hope it's not going to be something truly horrible, like Krenella."

Abbie found the book and brought it back to the boys' room, where her brothers and sisters were waiting nervously. "Okay," she said. "Let's see. This

baby's name will begin with *K*. If it's a boy he'll be"
—she counted down to the eleventh name on the
boys' *K* page—"Keegan."

"Not *too* bad," Hardy said slowly.

"And if it's a girl, she'll be . . . Kelly."

"Ooh, Kelly. That's pretty," said Candy.

"And normal," added Hannah.

"I hope it's a girl," said Jan.

"*I* hope it's a boy," said Woody.

"You know what?" said Bainbridge. "I just realized
something. I don't have to start a football team for
farm kids. No matter what the baby is, in a few
years, when Kelly or Keegan is walking, we'll have
eleven kids. That's enough for our *own* football team."

"Right," agreed Abbie with a happy sigh. "I'm glad
we'll be an eleven-kid family."

"Even if it ruins Mom's stairsteps," added Ira.

"Wait," said Bainbridge. "Correction. Not an
eleven-kid family."

"What then?" asked Woody. "You don't mean . . .
more twins?"

"Nope," replied Bainbridge. "I mean an eleven-kid,
one-pet family."

# CHAPTER ELEVEN
# *ZSA ZSA* or *ZURIEL*

Abbie thought it was fitting that the twins were the ones who found the Rossos' pet. They were the biggest animal lovers of all, and they were also the ones who were most concerned about homeless animals. It happened the very day after Mrs. Rosso had announced her surprising news and not long before she was to drive Abbie and her brothers and sisters to the pound.

"Faustine! Gardenia!" called Mrs. Rosso. "Would one of you run to the end of the driveway and get the mail, please?"

The twins went together, of course, talking excitedly about what kind of dog they might find at the pound.

"Shh!" Dinnie said as they neared the mailbox.

Faustine stopped talking. She thought she heard a tiny squeak. Then the noise came again, more loudly. "Mew."

The twins looked at each other. They ran to the ditch along the side of the road. "Kitty!" they called. "Here, kitty!"

"Mew. Mew!"

It didn't take long for the twins to find a tiny gray-and-white kitten huddled into a little ball near a puddle in the ditch. The kitten was wet and dirty and trembling.

"I'll get it!" cried Dinnie, sliding into the ditch.

"Be careful," said Faustine. "Don't let it bite you."

Dinnie approached the kitten slowly, talking to it in whispers. "You poor thing," she kept saying. "It's okay."

The kitten was too miserable to try to run away from Dinnie. It allowed itself to be picked up and then to be handed to Faustine before Dinnie scrambled out of the ditch. The twins took turns carrying it back to the farmhouse.

"Oh, good. You're back," said Mrs. Rosso, as they opened the screen door and came into the kitchen. "Let me just look at the mail, and then we'll leave for the pound."

"Oops," said Dinnie, as she realized they'd forgotten the mail.

"Oops," said Faustine.

And at that moment Mrs. Rosso saw the kitten. She gasped.

"We found it in the ditch," said Faustine.

"Someone must have abandoned it," Dinnie added.

"Well, for heaven's sake. Let's get it cleaned up." Mrs. Rosso set up an assembly line to wash, dry, feed, and cuddle the kitten.

By the time the kitten's fur was clean and its tummy was full, it was purring contentedly in Abbie's lap, eyes half-closed. The other kids had gathered.

"I guess we're going to keep it, aren't we?" said Abbie, glad that, for once, there was no question about whether they were allowed to.

"You want the kitten for your pet?" Mrs. Rosso asked. "This is it, you know. One baby, one pet. We aren't going to get a dog in *addition* to the kitten."

The Rosso kids held a silent meeting with their eyes. The kitten wasn't the same as a beagle or a poodle, and certainly not the same as a Doberman pinscher, but they wanted to keep it. After all, it was homeless, too. What did it matter whether they gave a home to a dog from the pound or a kitten from the ditch? Besides, who could turn away the rumbly ball of fur that was dozing in Abbie's lap?

"We want the kitten," Abbie said, speaking for her brothers and sisters as well as herself.

Mrs. Rosso nodded. "It's settled then. Who wants

to drive into town to buy a litter box and some food?"

Everyone did, but in the end Hannah, Hardy, Bainbridge, Jan, and Ira went, while Abbie, Candy, Woody, and the twins stayed with the kitten. They cuddled it and talked to it until it was exhausted and fell sound asleep, its front paws hanging over one side of Abbie's lap and its tail hanging over the other.

The kitten was wide awake by the time the others returned with two bags of cat supplies. As Abbie watched it frisk daringly around the kitchen, she thought, You'd never know that just a few hours ago this kitty was lost in a muddy ditch. Now it looks as if it owns our kitchen.

"Come here, kitty," said Jan. "You want to play with your toys? Look what we bought for you." She tossed a rubber mouse across the floor, and the kitten went skidding after it.

"Hey, it likes its toy!" exclaimed Jan.

"We better decide whether the kitten is a boy or a girl," said Candy. "Then we won't have to call it 'it.'"

"We need a name for it, too," said Hannah.

Dinnie picked the kitten up and examined it. "I can't tell if it's a boy or a girl," she said. "It's too young. We'll have to wait a couple of weeks until it's older."

"How are we going to name it?" asked Hardy. "We *have* to know whether it's a boy or a girl."

Bainbridge frowned. "Let's go outside and think about this. It's too hot in here."

Jan scooped the kitten up, and she and the rest of the kids marched through the screen door, which closed with a bang behind the last one, and out to the oak tree where Sally was buried. They sat in an untidy group. Hardy untied one of his sneakers and dangled the lace in front of the kitten, watching it bat it back and forth.

Abbie gazed around at her brothers and sisters and thought that they didn't look a thing like the New York kids who'd moved to the country almost a year ago. Those kids had been worried about pollution and muggers and cockroaches. They hadn't known a rose from a daffodil. The kids sitting under the oak tree were relaxed, slightly dirty (except for Ira), and not worried about much at all, except maybe bee stings. Or whose room the new baby would sleep in. They'd raised a nestful of birds, survived a snowstorm, and discovered a secret room in their house.

It was thoughts such as those that gave Abbie the courage to say, "I've got an idea about naming the kitten."

"What?" asked the others.

"I was just thinking that the ten of us haven't turned out too badly. Think of everything that's happened this year. We started at new schools and made new friends and had adventures. And we did it all with names like Dagwood and Calandra."

"And Bainbridge," added Bainbridge.

"Right," said Abbie. "So maybe Mom knows what she's doing. Or maybe not. But I think we should take the kitten's name from *What Shall We Name the Baby?* That way we won't have to argue over the name, and Mom would be flattered if we used the book. And it would be nice to flatter her since she did finally let us get a pet."

The Rosso kids considered this.

At last Bainbridge said importantly, "Abbie, do you move that we name the kitten from *What Shall We Name the Baby?*"

"Yes," replied Abbie. "I do."

"I second the motion," said Candy.

"All those in favor say aye," instructed Bainbridge.

"Aye," said Abbie, Bainbridge, Candy, Woody, Hardy, Faustine, Dinnie, Hannah, Ira, and Jan.

"Those opposed?"

Silence.

"Go get the book," said Bainbridge.

Abbie retrieved the book from the house and opened it to the *L* pages.

"Hey," said Candy, "what if Mom and Dad have *another* kid, after Kelly or Keegan? Or what if they have twins again? We better not use up either one of the twelfth *L* names."

"That's true," Abbie agreed. "But then we're not really using Mom's system."

"We don't know how many kids might be in our family one day, though," Candy pointed out.

"Well, we know one thing. There probably won't be twenty-six," Hannah said. "Let's start at the back of the book and give the kitten a Z name."

"The last Z name," Ira added. "Whatever it is. There probably aren't very many of them."

"Okay," said Abbie. "We'll look up the last boy's Z name and the last girl's Z name. When we know what the kitten is, we'll give it the right one."

Abbie opened the book gingerly. She was almost afraid to look. "Well," she said, "guess what. If it's a girl—Zsa Zsa."

"Zsa Zsa! That's cute!" exclaimed Jan.

"And if it's a boy—Zuriel."

"Oh, weird," muttered Hannah.

"Not weirder than Eberhard," said Hardy.

"What's going on out here?"

The Rosso kids looked up to see their mother crossing the farmyard.

"Mom, meet Zsa Zsa or Zuriel," said Abbie, holding up the kitten.

She explained how they had arrived at the names, and Mrs. Rosso began to look teary-eyed. "What a nice idea," she said.

"Don't get too carried away," Faustine cautioned

her, grinning. "If you and Dad have twins again, then we get to have a dog, too."

"Oh, brother," said Mrs. Rosso, shaking her head.

"Let's see. A dog," said Abbie. "What would we name it?"

"Second to last *Y* names," Hardy replied.

"And those," said Abbie, thumbing through the book, "are Yvette and Yule."

"Yule!" cried Hardy, choking. "You know something? I'm glad I'm named Eberhard!"

"And I'm glad I'm named Dagwood," said Woody.

"Well, I'll tell you something," Mrs. Rosso spoke up. "I'd love all you kids no matter what you were named."

"Even if we were John and Jim and Sue and Sally and not in alphabetical order?" asked Ira.

"Even then."

Ira sighed with contentment. His brothers and sisters turned look-alike freckled faces to Zsa Zsa or Zuriel and smiled at their first pet.

Ten kids, one pet, and a new baby on the way. Mrs. Rosso sighed with contentment too.